# The Gentleman Lion
# and Other Stories

*Martin Jones*

Copyright© 2022 Martin Jones
ISBN: 978-81-8253-872-6

First Edition: 2022
Rs. 200/-

Cyberwit.net
HIG 45 Kaushambi Kunj, Kalindipuram
Allahabad - 211011 (U.P.) India
http://www.cyberwit.net
Tel: +(91) 9415091004
E-mail: info@cyberwit.net

No part of this book may be reproduced or transmitted in any form or by any means, electronic, mechanical, photocopying, or otherwise, without the express written consent of Martin Jones.

This is a work of fiction. Names, characters, places and incidents eitherare the product of the author's imagination or are used fictitiously, and any resemblance to actual persons, living or dead, business establishments, events or locales, is entirely coincidental.

Illustration by Angelika Steckley

Printed at Repro India Limited.

To my family and friends who have
kept the laughter going through the years.

*Think Deeply. Dream Mightily*
- Norman Legrand

# Contents

*Meeting the Payzaks* 7

*Don't I Know You from Somewhere?* 22

*Brothers* 27

*The Far Shore* 42

*Dream Mightily* 55

*On the Ottawa Express* 72

*Waiting for the Assassins* 81

*The Detective and The Magician* 88

*Long Journey* 99

*The Music Solarium* 113

*The Gentleman Lion* 119

## Meeting the Payzaks

I am always late to the airport. It is a foolish thing, but I have a great fear of wasting time. I squeeze in as much work as I can before the taxi arrives. When I should be pulling up to Terminal Three of Toronto's Pearson Airport and paying the driver, I am standing at the front door of my apartment, waiting for the car to appear.

This day was no different. By the time I was in the airport and printing the boarding pass for my flight to Las Vegas, I feared the gate was about to close. I hustled through security and then American immigration and ran as fast as my weary lungs would take me to the gate.

Fortunately, the Vegas flight was delayed and I found a seat in the waiting area near the flight desk. I was breathing heavily from the run and only gradually became aware of a man arguing with an attendant.

"I don't see why I should," he was saying. "I am a frequent flyer with a platinum card." The man was in his forties, thin and medium-height, balding in front and bristling with irritation. A younger woman stood beside him, glancing to the side, looking uncomfortable. It was obvious she wished the man would shut up and sit down.

The attendant stared at him, sharp-faced. "Sir, you and your wife are on stand-by. We will call you when seats become available."

"Unbelievable," the man said. He turned away from the counter, his wife following. He said it again: "Un-fucking-believable," this time drawing out the syllables. "This world is going downhill so damned fast …" They stood behind me and I heard them quietly arguing. "Can't you get along for once?" said the woman. "If it's not this flight, we can take another."

"We are not people who wait. Other people wait, not us." Apparently, that was the end of the argument, which was followed by heavy, irritated breathing, tinged with the smell of gin.

I was glancing down at my tablet, opening a detective novel that I had downloaded for the flight, when the desk attendant called out, "Harold and Amber Payzak."

A few seconds later, a loud burst of anger erupted at the desk. "I don't fly economy, only business class. I was very clear about that."

"Captain," the attendant called out to the flight crew as it passed the desk. "Would you please speak to Mr. Payzak."

The captain, looking tall and smart in his blue uniform with the gold stripes on the wrist, glared at the man and asked: "What is the problem, sir?"

Payzak put his hands on his waist, elbows out, and drew himself up so that he was almost eye-level with the captain. "This is intolerable. First, I am a frequent flyer with a platinum loyalty card and I should not have to wait for a seat assignment. Finally, when we get our seats, they are in economy class. I never travel economy."

For a few moments the pilot said nothing, just stared at the man, then said quietly: "You will take what you get, sir. And you will be happy with it." The captain turned about and headed for the gate as scattered applause rose from a few near-by passengers; justice of a sort had been dispensed.

When boarding time came, I took my aisle seat in the plane, sat back and relaxed. Then the Payzaks entered the plane. Amber scanned her boarding pass and walked toward me. "Can I get past you, please. I have the middle seat." I stood in the aisle to let her pass and we sat down. I couldn't help but glance at her as she fiddled with her purse. She was a good-looking woman in her thirties, taller than average with short dark hair and a deep tan.

When I looked up, Payzak was standing a few metres away, arguing with a flight attendant. "My wife and I have to sit together." He looked down at me. "You, out of my seat. Move." I stared back at him, and then the harried-looking flight attendant said to me: "Sir, do you mind switching seats so this gentleman can sit with his wife."

I always book an aisle seat when I fly Economy. I'm a large man, six-foot-four, and it can be damned uncomfortable sitting in middle and window seats. So, I said, "I'm happy to move, as long as I have an aisle seat."

"I'm afraid there are no aisle seats left," said the attendant.

"This is unacceptable," Payzak announced, but was unable to say more. The captain came striding down the gangway. "What is all this racket about?" Then he saw Payzak standing in the aisle, glaring back at him. "You," the captain said. "I should have known. What's your problem now?"

"My wife and I are seated apart."

"Oh, really? I want you off my plane."

"What?"

"Take your luggage …" he jerked his thumb toward the exit, "… and get out."

Payzak let loose a loud sigh and ordered his wife: "Let's go." She stood up and squeezed past me. I wanted to say: "You don't have to go. You're not the one being thrown off." She must have read my mind, because as she stepped into the aisle, she leaned toward me and said: "You don't understand." And then they were gone.

\*

I had never been to Vegas before, and I liked it, at least at first. I am a consulting engineer and my work involves the structural integrity of large buildings. I was in Vegas to help bring down a structure, a large and ancient apartment building that for generations had housed folks who live and labour in Vegas, the working people who cook the food, make the beds, keep the elevators running and the gaming spaces clean. This was a four-day job and it involved no more than re-checking the calculations and inspecting the preparations and then, on Thursday, being on hand to witness the collapse of the old structure.

I have worked on many demolitions over the years, but there was something about this particular job that left me with an odd sense of loss. I had walked through the building a few times, had inspected every floor and been struck by the care that the architect and builders had put into the structure. The ceilings were higher, the walls thicker and the rooms larger than in buildings today. It seemed to me the people who had constructed this apartment were not trying to make a fast buck, that they genuinely cared about the residents who would live there.

I watched from a distance with the work crew as the explosives went off and the building began at first to tremble and shake, and then slowly, very slowly, the top slipped a few feet. There was a long pause, and then, all at once, the entire structure imploded into a deafening collapse and a few seconds later dust spewed high in the air.

The next morning, a Friday, I woke with plans to explore the city and its sights and try my hand at some games of chance. I walked up and down Las Vegas Boulevard that day, exploring famous hotels I had read about, the Luxor, the Bellagio, the Mirage and Grand, and playing quarter-dollar slots and a few rounds of Blackjack. On Saturday, I took a taxi north to the Vegas of the movies, the original gambling strip on Fremont Street. In some ways, I enjoyed that more. But by the late afternoon, fatigue and sadness pulled at me. I was becoming satiated, not on pleasure, but on its empty promise.

Walking south, I found a coffee shop, a room with half a dozen tables, not a place that big time gamblers would notice, unless they had lost everything and were stranded in the city. I sat at the back and ordered coffee, and for a few moments, closed my eyes to the world. It had been fun at first, walking aimlessly around casinos, but sitting here, alone with a coffee, I felt relief.

I heard the scrape of a chair and the sounds of someone putting items on a table. I wasn't sure at first, when my eyes opened, but the woman sitting a few feet away seemed to be Amber Payzak. She was examining the menu, and her purse and a book lay on the table. She did not recognize me when she looked up at me briefly, and normally I would have said nothing, but curiosity got the better of me. "Ms. Payzak?" I asked.

She glanced at me again, then stared, puzzled. "I'm sorry. Do I know you?"

"We sat together on the plane to Vegas, at least briefly. You left before we took off."

"Oh, yes?" She inspected me some more. I tend to think of myself as a good-looking man in his thirties, but I confess that my hair is receding, the black in my beard is fading and I'm almost 52. Except for my height, I am not someone a young woman would remember.

"You have a good memory," she said. "I've done my best to forget about that. We were lucky to get a later flight."

"My apologies for bringing it up. I was sorry to see what happened."

There was a long pause, and then she apologized to me for her husband's behavior. I shrugged and said it didn't bother me. She asked if I would like to sit with her. I came over and introduced myself as Len Argyle, and for a few moments we talked pleasantries, about which hotel the other was staying at and if either of us had enjoyed luck at the casinos. It seemed, though, that gambling interested neither of us.

"Not like my husband,' she said. "The slots and blackjack are all he thinks about when we're here. It's impossible to drag him away."

"I hope he wins more than he loses."

The waitress had come with a coffee and there was a silence as she put it down. I ordered a refill. Amber took a sip and said, "No. He's a big loser, but it doesn't matter."

"Why not?"

"You didn't recognize him, did you? On the plane?" I must have had a curious blank look on my face because she went on, "Three years ago, my husband and I won the lottery. Not a small win, two or three million dollars, but a huge win, tens of millions. The newspapers called him the Lumber Yard Lotto King."

Big lottery winners are so rare that you cannot help but look in amazement when you meet one. Then the reference to the lumber yard twigged my memory. I recalled a news item about a lottery winner, a likeable guy who had grown up in foster homes but had lifted himself from poverty and now owned a big lumber and hardware store. "I recall the guy was a committed church-goer," I said, "and planned to give his money away to charities and friends. Was that him?"

"That's Harold all right. He is basically a good-hearted man. That is one of the things I love about him. He had big plans to help others."

"And did he?"

She shook her head and gave a brief laugh. "Once the money was in his hands, it was like he went right down a rabbit hole with it. He could not bear to part with a penny if it was for anyone but himself. And believe me, he made a lot of promises, to our priest, to our friends, to my family, to a bunch of charities and they're all waiting.So, now we own three homes and five cars we don't need and every night he comes home drunk from strip joints."

The story's sadness left me searching for words. Finally, I said "But it must be nice having all that money."

"Who doesn't want to be rich? But not like this." She asked if I would like anything because she was going to order another coffee. I thanked her but declined.

There was a long silence and I began feeling uncomfortable. Then she asked: "What is it about men? Why is Harold so bent on self-destruction?"

The questions startled me and I shrugged. "I don't know."

She stared and asked: "What's your story, Len? Why would anyone come to Vegas alone?"

I told her why I was there and gave her my business card. She looked over the card and said aloud, "L. G. Argyle, Engineering Consultant." Then asked: "Are you married? Do you have kids?"

She said this as a matter of genuine interest. There was a straightforward honesty to Amber, a self-confidence, that I was beginning to like. "I have a daughter, grown up, with two kids of her own," I said.

"And your wife?"

"I'm a widower."

"Oh, I'm sorry to hear that."

"Don't be. It was a few years ago. I'm fine."

I don't remember precisely what we talked of next, but it was mainly about her life and extended family. She had been a nurse, but had not worked since the lottery win, and was still hoping to have children. There was a warmth in the way she spoke. Then she said, "You probably wonder why I don't leave my husband, when he can be such a jackass."

"No. It's not my business."

"Other people wonder, Len. I know in his heart he is a good man. It's my job to help the good man in Harold get home again."

I simply nodded in agreement. I was becoming attracted to this young woman with the pretty face and the dark tan. I could tell she really did not care that much about money, but she did care about Harold. The man she loved had wandered into a dark zone and she was going to bring him home.

I offered to take her back to Las Vegas Boulevard in a taxi, but she was happy sitting there by herself, so I said how much I had enjoyed speaking with her and left. That night, as I ate alone in an Italian restaurant, then wandered back to my hotel room and lay on the bed, I thought of Amber. There was something about her that reminded me of Vanessa, my wife. I had told Amber that she had died a few years ago, but the truth was that it had only been 18 months and I was a long way from getting over it. It had all happened so fast. She left for work early on a Friday morning and been killed by a drunk driver a few minutes later. How could anyone be that drunk so early in the morning? The driver was in his early twenties. He will be out of jail soon. All such a waste.

Knowing I will never see Vanessa again is the hardest thing about this. I find myself through the day thinking, "I must remember to tell Vanessa that joke I heard…" or "I'll surprise her this evening with a bottle of the white wine she loves." Then, I remember. You would think I'd be over that stage by now, but I am nowhere close.

Maybe for that reason I thought it might be nice to see Amber again, just to talk with a good-hearted woman once more, yet how would that happen? We did not exactly move in the same circles, and besides, since Vanessa's passing, I have come to lead a solitary life and rarely meet anyone. In fact, maybe a life that was too solitary. My daughter has warned me about becoming isolated from family and friends. I run my consulting business from home and don't get out to building sites as often as I should. My chief exercise is solitary hiking. And I watch way too much television, alone. I did wonder, if I had let things get this bad, how was I going to survive retirement? Maybe I would end my days marinating in whiskey and dying too soon, like so many lonely, retired men.

Those were dreary thoughts. The advantage of being far from home, though, is that it gives you a fresh perspective to consider your life.

I was booked on a flight out of Las Vegas on Monday morning, so I woke early Sunday with a full day on my hands. It was a beautiful sunny morning, and I walked about the downtown and could not get over the size of the crowds on the early morning streets.

In Vegas, almost everyone is on vacation and folks are just looking for fun, which makes it easy to talk to strangers. I spoke with a garrulous priest who was collecting money for the down and out folks of the city. He spoke about the fresh-faced optimists who arrive in Vegas looking for work or for a big win at the casinos, and soon find themselves penniless. I liked the man, but then again, he may have been just a hustler collecting his gambling stake. Anyone can put a collar on backwards and hold up a tin can with a sign reading "For the Poor." I preferred to think he was for real.

I talked to other people that day. Two guys at a bar, one from Iowa and the other from Los Angles, complained how tough it was to survive on gambling. "There hasn't been a big win for months," the fellow from Iowa said and the man from California speculated that the casinos were altering the odds.

Toward 5 pm I was sitting on a restaurant terrace, nursing a beer. I was thinking what a bizarre artificial city this was, at least the parts of Vegas that tourists see. There is a neon phoniness to it that repels but at the same time thrills you with such extraordinary novelty that is hard to pull yourself away, even to go to bed for the night. It is not one thing but everything, the frantic energy and seductive lights of the big gambling halls, the endless movement of wide-eyed crowds, the sweeping, jumbled architectural excess of the hotels and casinos. It is way the huge fountain at the Bellagio can transfix a person and the sight of the six towers of Caesar's Palace stretching off into the late-night darkness.

It is the excess of everything. And everywhere, in the passing mobile billboards advertising escorts, in the endless pamphlets for strip clubs and whores that are tossed on the streets, in the self-conscious stride of women on the make moving hawk-eyed through the hotel lobbies and bars, there is the omnipresent promise of sex.

When my cell phone rang suddenly, I figured it was something to do with work, but it wasn't. It was Amber Payzak. She sounded happy; she and Harold were in a limo returning from a visit to the Grand Canyon. They had had a wonderful day. Would I like to join them for dinner at their hotel, say around 8 pm?

Of course, I said "Yes".

The restaurant was more glamorous than anything I had seen so far, designed with an elegant oak veneer. The maître d' led me toward the back, past a fire pit that did little to alleviate the dim lighting, and then motioned towards a table in an alcove, where I saw the Payzaks.

Harold stood up, smiling, and we shook hands. "It's always great to meet someone from home," he said. Amber mentioned how enjoyable our time in the coffee shop had been. She seemed to think my being a structural engineer who occasionally destroyed old buildings was a big deal, and I did nothing to correct her.

"I hear I was rude to you in the plane. I apologize. Too much to drink in the airport, I'm afraid," Harold said. I told him that if it had happened, I did not remember and soon we were laughing and talking about Vegas. We ordered our wine and then our dinners. I noticed that Harold stayed with his water and did not order alcohol, which was likely at Amber's request. He was a thoroughly different man than on the airplane. Polite, thoughtful, a good conversationalist. It was easy to see the toughness and intelligence of the young man, of the orphan with no advantages, who had made his way successfully in the world before his big lottery win.

We talked about many things, about the Grand Canyon and the beauty of the desert, about Toronto's professional sports teams. Harold was a devotee of motivational writers and we shared our thoughts on that.

Amber said little; she seemed to me to be relieved and happy to witness her husband being his old self and talking enthusiastically to someone who took an interest in his ideas.

We finished off with coffees and they insisted on picking up the dinner bill. Then Harold stood up and asked: "How would you like to have fun tonight, Len? I know a bar not far away where only the locals go. It's a great place."

Amber's expression soured in a moment. "Let's just go back to our suite, honey. We all have a flight to catch tomorrow morning."

"I've been a good guy all day. It's time for some fun." He looked at me and winked. Without meaning to, I glanced at Amber. She frowned and shook her head, as if to say, "Don't encourage him."

Harold tossed his napkin on the table. "Well, I'm off, alone or with you, Len." It happened so quickly I was taken by surprise. Amber said: "I can't stop him. Will you stay with him tonight and keep him from drinking too much?"

What could I say, but yes? "Promise me," she said, "promise me that he won't get so drunk he does something stupid." I promised her and then walked quickly after him as he exited the restaurant.

Harold had been right about the bar; it was a lively place with a great vibe and rocking country music and the patrons all knew him. They were laughing together at the bar and Harold was draining two straight vodkas for every beer that I could drink. After a couple more drinks, I tried to convince it was time to leave, to get back to our hotels. He laughed in my face and insisted I join him and his friends at another bar, close by, one that turned out to be a lot shabbier than the first.

We all drank and talked some more, and Harold suddenly shifted into that stage of drunkenness in which a mania takes over your thoughts and you talk way too fast. He began a story about racing off the coast of Florida in cigarette boats, those long, thin performance craft with ridiculously extended bows that move at impossibly high speeds. They burn hundreds of dollars of fuel with every trip, he was saying, and you can outrun any police craft on the ocean. "But you have to know what you are doing or you could flip and die in a moment."

Folks were hanging on every word, yet I was sure he was repeating stories others had told him. Someone asked how Harold could afford to own a cigarette boat and that started him talking about the millions he had made through shrewd investing and began tossing out names of good investments. People listened, though I sensed after a while Harold's talk of money was wearing thin. Soon, a good-looking woman was standing beside him, pretending to look enthralled. Two guys standing at the bar beside me were snickering; she was a local hooker, they said, a particularly nasty one. I walked over to him and grabbed his shoulder and said: "Look, buddy, it's late, almost 1:30," but he no longer seemed to remember who I was.

I tried again to get his attention but he wheeled around quickly. "Go to hell. This is none of your goddamn business."

Now the bartender was talking to him. "Go with your friend, mister.

You've had a good night but that's enough." Harold glared back a moment. "What's it to you? Just give me another goddamn vodka." The man stared at Harold, then picked up the bottle and poured out a shot and Harold greedily drank it.

By now I was feeling ill and sat down alone at a table, woozy and fatigued. I considered what to do. I had promised Amber I would get her husband home safely but short of kidnapping him… Then I figured why not. I was a lot bigger than Harold. I would just call a cab and drag him into it. But I was feeling so tired, I may have dozed off for a bit, because when I looked again toward the bar, Harold was gone. He must have left alone because the tavern was full and the hooker now had her arm draped around someone else. I looked about the bar for him and then checked outside but he was nowhere to be seen.

I wondered what to do next and decided I should phone and tell Amber what happened. With luck, Harold might already be on his way to his hotel. I took out my cell and tapped on the number that Amber had called me on earlier that day, but all I got was Harold's voice mail. Fortunately, their hotel was on the way to mine, so I flagged a cab and took it to straight to their hotel. But I must have struck the night receptionist as a crazy drunk, because he refused to tell me the couple's room number or the phone number for their suite. I scribbled something on paper and gave it to him, then left.

Around 5 am my phone woke me. "Do you know what happened?" a woman said before I could even speak. "I'm in the hospital with Harold. He's been shot." Amber was struggling to sound calm. "He came back to the hotel half an hour ago, drunk, with a gunshot wound in his shoulder. What happened?"

"I don't know" I said. "I stayed with him till almost 2 am. But he was out of control, Amber, off in his own drunken world and didn't remember who I was. I looked away for a moment and he was gone."

"Gone? How could he be gone?" There was a pause, and then she almost shrieked into the phone, "You useless old man. I asked you to do one thing for me and you failed." There was another long pause as Amber breathed with irritation into the phone. "I have to go." She hung up.

I did not see Amber and Harold in the waiting area at the Las Vegas airport. But I saw them board after the rest of us were seated. They were at the front of the plane, in business class, but the curtain had not yet been drawn and I could see them from where I was sitting. Harold looked to be in great pain, barely awake, and his sleeve was torn off and his shoulder heavily bandaged. Amber helped him into a seat and sat down beside him.

I waited until we were airborne and the seatbelt lights switched off, then stood up and walked to the front of the plane. I wanted to explain what had happened and did not care that I was trespassing into business class. "How is he?" I asked Amber and then glanced at Harold. "How's the shoulder?" Amber looked up at me, and softly, as if she wanted no one else to hear, said: "Please Len, not now." At that same moment Harold gazed up and croaked, "Hey Len. How the hell you doing, buddy?" With a sudden rage that surprised me, Amber snapped: "Oh, shut up Harold. You're still drunk."

I walked back to my seat and looked at the list of movie offerings; none looked appealing. The plane landed after what felt like an interminable flight, then we waited another twenty minutes at the gate. Eventually, four police officers boarded the plane and took Harold and Amber away. It looked like the Vegas police department had contacted their Toronto counterparts and that Harold might truly be in trouble.

I saw them again, speaking with police at customs. Without thinking, I stopped and stared. Harold looked up, sadly. But Amber's gaze on me was one of undisguised contempt. Then she rolled her eyes and looked away. I figured I would not see her again.

At home, there was work waiting on my desk, urgent enough that I did not bother to unpack. I sat down to tackle it, but an hour later, my mind began to wander. From time to time, I miss Vanessa beyond reason and long to see her smile and hear her laugh and soft voice. Even if it were only once, even if it were just to say goodbye. This night wasn't like those times. This felt far worse.

I tried to shake the grief and found myself reflecting on Harold and his journey – how he had gone from being the hard-working young man who built a business to the reckless drunk I had witnessed in Vegas. I asked myself if I were a younger man, would I behave any differently if someone gave me endless money and freedom? Maybe not; maybe I would become even worse. Maybe you would too.

As I sat reflecting, I considered the apartment building we had just demolished. There was a strange power to the image of that collapsing structure. It stayed in my mind all afternoon and into the evening as I watched the late-night news on television. The memory of the apartment was still in my thoughts at midnight when I took a tumbler of Scotch out to the balcony and gazed over the city below. I couldn't stop thinking about the roof of that old building, and how, at first, it looked like things were happening in slow-motion. Then, there was that long pause before the inevitable collapse.

## Don't I Know You from Somewhere?

On a steaming August night, so humid and slick the shirt sticks to shoulders and back, a man in a brown suit hurries up the narrow street and flags a passing taxi.

The cab brakes screech and through the open passenger window, the white-haired driver shouts: "Where are you going?"

The man is going north, about two miles, and the driver motions him into the back seat. But when he gets in, a woman is already sitting there, directly behind the driver. She leans forward, toward the old man. "This is outrageous. You don't let someone in the cab without asking me."

The driver shrugs. "What's the guy to do? The streetcars have stopped for the night."

The younger man glances over and smiles at the woman. She is a bit younger than him, early thirties he imagines. He likes the way her anger has lit up her dark, blue eyes and made her toss her long brown hair. She has been drinking, he guesses, as she awkwardly moves a black purse to her left side. The upper button of her blouse is undone and he notices the silver pendant hanging from her necklace.

"Don't worry about me," he says. "I will sit quietly on my side."

"I'm angry at the driver, not you." She is irritated, still, the man hears something soft in her voice.

The car pulls into traffic and his mind drifts back to the long and pointless dinner he had just left. He sells flooring products, wholesale, and the retailer he was pitching over after-dinner drinks had no interest in what he had to offer, just wanted to drink and schmooze about nothing. The young man considers his to be one of those disappointing jobs that most people have. He could do better, he knows.

No one is speaking in the taxi. The young man glances out the window for a few moments, then turns to the woman and says, "It is so quiet tonight, even the houses look asleep."

She stares at him for several seconds, furrows her eyebrows. "Don't I know you from somewhere?"

The man peers at her. "You know …you're right. I do know you, but I can't remember where we met."

"It must have been years ago," she says. "Maybe a foreign city?"

He reflects for a moment. "I have the same feeling. Europe somewhere?"

"Maybe. I spent a year in Paris, after university."

"That's right," he says. "It's coming back. You were working …where?"

"I was studying French. But I worked part-time, in a hotel."

"Yes, of course. Mary, isn't it?"

She is startled by this. "Maria, actually. My god, you have a good memory. That was 12 years ago. I apologize; I can't remember your name."

"John," he says. The two remain quiet for several seconds. "Well, Maria. It is great to see you after all these years. And a bit strange too."

"Yes. Both those things."

There is silence as the cab slips narrowly past some parked cars. John asks: "Do you remember the place where we spent the afternoon?"

"I remember going somewhere with a man I just met. The House of Rodin?"

"Yes, the old house with the sculptures. That was memorable. I still think about that afternoon."

"Really? That's nice," Maria says.

"Do you remember how we ended up in Place Pigalle? We thought it would be fun to visit a cabaret."

She thinks a moment. "It sounds familiar." Maria moves closer to him. The driver stops for a red light, and casts a puzzled glance in the rear-view mirror, just as a police cruiser flashes by. The light turns green and the taxi moves on.

"You know, Maria, I remember more now. We walked down from Montmartre to the Seine. It was a warm night like this, except there were so many people about. We followed those narrow streets beneath the stars for two hours, sometimes stopping to say a few words with strangers." He thinks a moment. "There was a couple who invited us to sit with them and share their wine. Do you remember that?"

"I think I vaguely remember that. God, it sounds so beautiful." Maria smiles at him, then offers tentatively: "John, you're a nice man. Why did I never see you again?"

"I was in Paris for only a few days. I gave you my home phone number and said we should get-together when you got back."

"I have no memory of that. But then again, it was a long time ago."

"Just think how strange life is, Maria. Maybe if you had called me, our lives would've turned out differently."

"That's a funny thought. I hope it would've been a better life."

He considers this for a moment. "It's tough out there in the world, isn't it?"

"Somehow, you expect life to be better than it is. It seems like so much work at times and not much to look forward to."

The driver turns onto a side street and the car moves slowly ahead. "What number was that again, ma'am?"

"One forty-seven." She gestures over the front seat. "There on the right, the duplex with the outside staircase."

The taxi draws up to the curb and stops in front of the house. Maria lifts her purse and opens it, but John places his hand over hers. "I am going a lot further. It makes sense for me to pay."

"Are you sure?"

"Yes. It was great meeting you again, Maria." Maria sits, not moving.

"Ma'am?" asks the driver.

"Just a few seconds, driver." She smiles at John. It is a long smile, and then she reaches into her purse and takes out a pen and some paper and begins to write. She hands it to John. "This is my phone number. Text or call me sometime."

John studies the paper briefly. "I will."

"Don't let another twelve years go by." She opens the car door and pauses. She turns toward John. "Maybe our lives can still turn out differently."

"Maybe they can."

The taxicab pulls away from the curb as John watches Maria walk toward the house and the wrought-iron staircase. The cab pulls away and at the yield sign at the end of street, slows and comes to a stop. The driver turns and looks at John. "That was quite something, meeting a girl you haven't seen in 12 years. "

"Yes. Quite something."

"One for the books," says the old man. "Paris, that's a place I've always wanted to see. Is it as beautiful as they say?"

"Oh, definitely," says John. The taxicab pulls onto a main street and John wonders about Maria. He is drawn by her dark blue eyes and the soft way she has of speaking. He likes what she said – that maybe their lives can still turn out differently. Perhaps he will phone her in two or three days.

But then again, should he really do that? After all, he has never been to Paris, never laid eyes on Maria before. And as he considers this, he wonders what Maria might be thinking now as she undresses for bed. He imagines her putting a finger on the silver pendant hanging outside her blouse, the one in the shape of the letter M and realizing, suddenly, how easy it might be for a stranger to guess that your name is Mary … or Maria. Or maybe she will not be that surprised, for she must realize that the nighttime walk down from Montmartre was not her memory, only something that seems like a memory worth having.

## Brothers

On a frigid evening in March, Eddy arrived in our little town without notice. My phone rang and there was a long pause, followed by Eddy's voice, more gravely and laboured than I remembered: "Scotty, it's the Reever. Do you mind if an old guy pitches up on your couch?"

I had not seen Eddy in years. He lived in Toronto, a four-hour drive to the west of us. Josie, my wife, had said she never wanted my older brother in our lives again, but it was difficult to say 'no.' Eddy never had money and he likely had no place to stay. I wanted to consult with Josie, but on that Friday evening she was at a movie with friends. I said sure, he was welcome to stay.

"Ah, that's kind of you," came the sound of his voice, with the faint twang of a Newfoundland accent, though much faded. I waited through the long silence. "Would you mind picking me up at the bus station?"

"Not at all."

"I'm afraid my pension cheque is lost in the mail," he said.

I told him I understood.

Eddy was waiting outside the station, a single suitcase in hand, no longer the tall, erect figure I remembered. He was dressed in a worn, wool great coat, and he stooped in the dark windy chill, glancing nervously about as if hoping, or perhaps fearing, someone might recognize him. I called to Eddy and he walked over to the car, opened the back door and lifted a soiled, brown leather suitcase gently onto the seat and climbed into the front.

He stuck out his palm. "Hello, old son." I smiled and shook his hand, and in the neon reflection from the bus stop café, I noticed the broken red veins in his raw face and along his nose. I was not surprised;

I had heard from a friend that Eddy's drinking was getting worse. As the car pulled away from the curb, he said, "Nothing's the same anymore, is it Scotty?"

"What do you mean, Eddy?"

"No respect for an old guy. They don't even give you enough to live on. My pension from hockey barely buys a cup of coffee and what the government pays doesn't even cover rent. Not like the old days, eh Scotty."

"Oh yeah? How's that?"

"Back then, players' salaries were just starting to get good. Even an average Joe was making more money than he'd ever seen before. Those were some good times."

"Still going on about all the old shit," I said.

Eddy barked back. "Why not. I got a right to."

"Okay, okay, let's cool it." I immediately regretted what I had said.

If you are old enough to recall the early years of NHL expansion, you may remember Eddy. He was a marginal player for most of his career but popular with fans for his hard-hitting style of play and telegenic TV interviews. You may also remember his nickname, Eddy "The Grim Reever" Reeves. In his fourth season with the National Hockey League, Eddy surprised everyone by emerging as a player so hard-charging and relentless that when he carried the puck over the opposing blue line, defencemen scrambled in terror to stop him.

That fourth season was effectively his last. And if you remember Eddy, I bet you also know how his career ended.

Now, he asked: "Have you heard of the town of Hawkesbury?"

"I have," I said. It was one of the larger towns on the Ottawa River.

"Well, I am off tomorrow morning to visit Cousin Bernice."

With Eddy, a cousin could mean anything. "Do you need a ride?"

"Only if it's convenient."

"It's fine," I said.

"That's my brother. I can always count on you. But…"

"Yes?"

"What does Josie say?"

"She doesn't know you're here. We'll cross that bridge when we come to it."

I glanced over at him. He did not look reassured.

Eddy was my half-brother, older by 15 years; as a child, I hardly knew him. When I was three, he was 18 and playing his first season with the minor league Rochester Americans. By the time I was seven, he was suiting up with the NHL expansion team, the California Seals.

We arrived home and I made up a cot in our basement rec room and brewed two cups of decaf coffee for us. We talked a while, then Eddy began to nod off and went downstairs to sleep. I waited in the living room for Josie to arrive home. When she did, she listened patiently to me, then said: "Scotty, I asked you to keep him out of our lives."

"He's my brother, Josie. What am I supposed to do?"

She stared at me, her face tense with frustration. "One night only and then I want him gone."

Fortunately, Josie never remains angry for long. The next morning, she and Eddy were laughing over plates of bacon and eggs. He was telling her how he played golf with old men who paid his green fees so they could brag about knowing him. I guess that's one perk of having once been famous, but it would embarrass me.

It is 100 kilometres from our village near the St. Lawrence River to Hawkesbury, and Eddy was not meeting Bernice until the early afternoon, but I wanted to leave before noon so we could drive slowly and enjoy the countryside. He had his suitcase and I kidded him that he must know cousin Bernice awfully well or be incredibly cocky to think she would let him stay with her overnight.

"I don't think she's really my cousin, Scotty," he said as we started rolling. "She has my mother's name, Dwyer, so I figured we're cousins." There was a long pause. "I want you to meet her, Scotty. She has a lovely soul."

This seemed an odd sentiment coming from Eddy, who was normally a guy of blunt words and simple facts. But odder still, I thought, was that I had never known Eddy's mother's maiden name, or in fact much about her at all. I knew she had died – it had been suicide my father told me – when Eddy was 12. After that, our father had taken Eddy with him from the tiny Newfoundland outport of Wolf's Head to Toronto, where he met and married my mother.

"I never knew your mother's name, Eddy," I said. "I don't know much about her at all."

"I don't talk about her, Scotty. I get too upset. It wasn't fair what happened to her." Eddy's voice was rising. I was afraid I had set off one of his rants, but he quickly calmed down, adding merely, "My mother was too good for this world," and that was it. He said no more.

It was a beautiful day, sunny and chill, with the odd patch of snow on the ground. I don't remember the route we took that afternoon, because I drove almost randomly, heading east and occasionally north. Tidy farmhouses and barns nestled close to the roads, while fields and barren trees stretched over the brown hills and valleys.

We do not have a whole lot in common, Eddy and I, but we have hockey, and we talked about great hockey teams of the past as we drove along. I have hockey and Eddy to thank for whatever success I've enjoyed in life. I'm a former professor of business and now an administrator at a community college. That may not sound like much to some people, but I consider it a success for someone who grew up in a tough working-class neighborhood in Toronto. After Eddy was forced out of the sport, he came home and coached me and a few friends on the finer points of the game. He did such a great job teaching me that I eventually won an athletic scholarship to an Ivy League university.

I sometimes ponder all this. My life has been a rich one. I have Josie and our two children, both grown up but still close to us. I have work that I love. And then I look at Eddy's life, which seemed at times to be one defeat after another and I wonder how such unfairness in life is possible.

Eventually, Eddy and I ran out of things to talk about and focused our attention on the view. Slowly, I sensed that his mood was growing sullen. His face tightened into a grimace and his eyes seemed lost to inner thoughts. He blurted suddenly, "I've been thinking about Wolf's Head."

"What sort of thinking?"

He turned to me. "I'm afraid of death, Scotty."

"Eddy, what nonsense are you talking?"

"In Wolf's Head people talked crazy things."

"Stop it, Eddy." I knew where this was going because it had happened before. Back in Newfoundland, the family had belonged to an evangelical church where everyone but the members were going straight to hell. When Eddy's mother died by her own hand, she too was denounced as one of the "damned," which led to my father never stepping inside a church again. Eddy now turned and looked straight ahead. "Forget it." A few seconds later, he was pointing to a fox by the road and talking about the view. His dark mood had passed.

I was not paying attention to road signs, so I was surprised when the village of Dunvegan appeared before us. Just beyond the village limits lives a former student from my early days of teaching. His name is Rich Owens and he owns a gas station and restaurant. I stop there a couple of times a year to fill up and have a coffee and a chat. I pulled into the station, topped up my gas tank and then asked Eddy to come inside and meet the owner. But no, he wanted to sit in the car and wait.

Rich was there, as friendly and full of laughter as ever, but to my surprise, so was an old buddy, Shaun Costello. The two of us had grown up together in the same housing complex and Shaun had been one of the kids that my brother had coached. Shaun has always had a way about him that makes everyone like him, including Eddy. When he chose the priesthood as his life's vocation, no one was happier than my irreligious brother. "Just think of little Shaun as a priest," he told me. "Spreading all his happiness around."

Today, Shaun has a parish nearby. I asked him and Rich to come outside and say hi to Eddy, but when we exited the restaurant, my brother was gone. We walked around the station and looked up and down the road. There was no sign of him anywhere. Rich asked his staff if they had seen anything. A waitress said she was outside having a smoke when an older man, a big man, got out of the passenger seat of a car to have a talk with two local farm hands she knew. Then the three of them headed off in a Chevy truck.

"Those guys spend their Saturdays drinking in Hawkesbury," she said. Shaun let out a rueful laugh and remarked, "Just like the old Reever." I said good-bye to my friends and headed off. If I was fast enough, I could overtake their truck, but they must have been moving at a fair clip because I never did catch them.

This was the old Eddy that I had grown tired of, that my wife had barred from our lives. He had likely grown bored sitting in my car and told the farm workers he had once played in the NHL and they had invited him to go drinking with them. There were other occasions like this when Eddy's misbehavior threatened to ruin things. Josie and I still talk of the time we went off with Eddy and his second wife to a New Year's Eve party. We were in our mid-twenties then and were sitting in the backseat of Eddy's car when he suddenly pulled over to the curb. He announced he had to meet someone and abruptly got out of the vehicle and left. We waited while it grew bleak and cold in the dark car. Finally, I went looking for Eddy in the bars and restaurants along the street. Twenty minutes later, I found him sitting in a restaurant, staring angrily into space and drinking rye and ginger. He had forgotten all about us.

There are other stories I could tell you, like the one that ended with my brother being barred from our home. He was visiting and got roaring drunk on a Sunday afternoon, just before Josie's parents, sister and nieces arrived for dinner. Eddy, loud and clumsy, managed to break a vase, insult Josie's family and frighten the little girls. That was a very bad evening, one I prefer not to dwell on.

The "Eddy stories" seemed funny once, but now they only make me sad. I still do not know what to make of Eddy's behavior. A few years after his hockey career ended, he was working in a warehouse and injured himself. The doctor said there was no long-term damage to the brain, but I had to wonder because Eddy was never the same after that. Then again, his strange moods may have been the result of the terrible guilt he felt and brutal pounding that life had administered to him.

So here I am, thirty years on and once again looking for my brother, this time in Hawkesbury, one of the saddest places you can imagine. There was a paper plant here once and a few small factories; now they are mostly gone. Many of the ten thousand inhabitants are elderly and whatever they get up to in their spare moments, it is not patronizing the local bars, because the first few I checked out were almost empty. I had more luck down by the riverfront, where I found Eddy sitting in the corner of a pub with a gaggle of men and women. He was pumped up like a hip-hop artist on amphetamines, boasting of ancient triumphs. "Man, that was coolest goal I ever scored. The goalie was crouched low and I caught the net just over his left shoulder. No one could believe I found that tiny opening." Seeing me, he flashed a wide smile and turned to his new friends, suddenly raising his glass and splashing beer over the table. "Hey guys, here's my little brother, Scotty." I sat down and shook hands with folks, and Eddy went on, stuffed with bravado. "Give me a name from that time," he was saying, "and I probably knew the guy."

I glanced down the table and saw two of the older men snickering; they probably remembered my brother's exploits all too well. I caught Eddy's attention and asked what the hell he was doing. "You've got to meet Bernice in half an hour. You don't want to stink of beer." There was a flicker of attention, but it didn't register. He kept right on.

I got up and walked out to the street to catch some fresh air. I should not have expected anything different from Eddy. I thought how Bernice, whoever she was, was about to discover what Josie and I had learned, that you could never trust Eddy to follow through on anything.

I was outside that bar for maybe two minutes, when a wide, squat woman came towards me, huffing, her broad Irish face red with effort. "Mister, is it true your brother killed his wife and child?"

I sighed. I should have known someone would bring that up, eventually. "It was an accident. My brother would never harm anyone."

"Well, you better get back in, cause there's a big argument going on."

Inside, a man sitting beside Eddy, an ugly-faced drunk, was talking loudly to his friends. "Here's a guy who had it made. Eddy, you see, is traded to the Rangers and he and his wife and little kid..." He looked over at a sheep-faced Eddy and sneered, "You only had one kid to kill, didn't you Reeves?" Eddy looked back at him, unable to speak, as the man went on, "He's on a flight with his family from California to New York and the plane does a stop in Indianapolis to pick up passengers. And what does this asshole do? He's drunk and he flicks a lit cigarette between the seats."

I could not believe this was going on. I moved closer to this jerk and said tersely, "Leave my brother alone. It was an accident and it was long ago." But the guy ignored me. He stood up, his face screwed up in rage, and stared down at Eddy, who was looking away, mortified. He started to shout. "And you started a fire didn't you, killer? Your wife and kid chocked to death on the smoke. Pretty proud of yourself, eh Reeves." Two fists suddenly swung through the air and Eddy toppled back on his chair, landing loudly on the floor, a cut over his eye and his nose bleeding. Eddy's attacker was looming over him, shaking his fists, yelling, "Stand up and fight, you goddamn coward." Within seconds, four or five others jumped up and joined him, laughing and shouting at Eddy to fight back.

I stepped quickly between them and Eddy, almost screaming. "Back off you guys." Then I glared at the guy waving his fists around. "This is an old man. You got no bloody business punching him." I was taller than the attacker by half a foot, and he was drunk and none too steady on his feet. I got Eddy upright and across the barroom floor to the door without incident. The group at the table were whooping with laughter and I heard the guy who had hit Eddy shouting, "Get that loser out of here." There was a restaurant halfway down the block where we found a booth to sit down in.

Eddy took a couple of napkins and wiped the blood from his nose and rubbed the back of his head. "Why do people keep bringing up that old stuff, Scotty?" He had such a sad, broken look on his face I could hardly bear to look at him.

I shook my head. "I don't know, Eddy." I remembered how a week after the fire on the parked plane my grief-stricken brother laced his skates for the Rangers' opening game, stepped on the ice and was met by a wall of boos. He played that opening game but his performance was hopeless; he had nothing left inside him. What's more, the Ranger's management and the players just didn't want him around. That first spin with the Rangers was his last game in the big leagues.

The investigation of the aircraft fire began a week or so later. It turned out that Eddy had indeed started it with a lit cigarette. He and his wife had been drinking in the Los Angeles airport before departure and kept on imbibing during the flight. She was too inebriated to flee the fire and both she and the child had died of smoke inhalation. Fortunately, no one else on the plane had been harmed. Eddy was charged with something; I can't remember what it was. He was convicted, but was lucky, if you could call it that. The judge took pity on him and he spent only a year and a bit in jail. However, I know nothing of that period of his life. Eddy always refused to talk about it

I got Eddy, bloody nose and all, into the car and drove him to the hotel coffee shop where had arranged to meet Bernice. We arrived with five minutes to spare. Eddy went to the washroom to clean up, and I sat alone, ordering cups of coffee for the three of us, when I had a new worry. What if Bernice failed to show? If that happened, I knew Eddy would march out and buy a bottle of Canadian Club and it might be months, even years, before I saw him again.

"Are you Scotty?" I looked up to see a woman with frizzy black hair and a warm smile. She appeared to be in her late 50s. I stood up and shook her hand and introduced myself. She slid into the booth on Eddy's side. "I've heard so much about you. It's nice to finally meet you."

I had assumed Bernice was a new friend. But no, they had known each other for years. She laughed and said, "He considers my little house in the country to be his home. You know that saying, 'home is where they have to take you in?' Each time he shows up on my doorstep, I take him in and I never know how long he plans to stay."

Eddy came back from the washroom and the two of them hugged. Eddy kissed her on the cheek. "Isn't she great, Scotty," he said, and I agreed. We made small talk over coffee and then Eddy left with Bernice. I was relieved to leave too, to be in my car, heading home. And I was relieved for Eddy. He was right; Bernice did have a lovely soul.

Yet, as I drove on, I began reflecting on Eddy and the way he had laughed with Bernice. A happy man for once and I was happy for him, though I wondered how long this relationship would last. Some people's lives glow with good fortune; success trails after them wherever they venture, as if the gods have intervened to bless them. And then there are the Eddys of the world, singled out at random for disappointment and pain, whose lives become one great festering wound that never heals.

Everything after hockey was downhill for Eddy. Nothing ever worked out, whether it was jobs or marriages or places to live. He was always on the move, from one crummy apartment to another, always broke. Such was Eddy's life, but what was his great transgression? He was a simple soul who had never meant to do ill to anyone. Fifty years ago, he made one terrible mistake, but were not the consequences of that one error painful enough? Did the fates have to hound him down through the years? I hoped that maybe Eddy was finally going to get a break, to live in peace with a woman he obviously loved.

\*

I should have visited Eddy in the weeks that followed, but April is a busy time at college, even for administrators like me. In early May, Bernice phoned and told me Eddy did not have long to live. It was his heart, she said, the doctor had told her it had simply worn out, along with his liver and his lungs.

Could I come, she asked. And could I bring someone named Shaun for Eddy to talk to.

"What? Shaun Costello? Why?"

"To confess or something. I don't know. Eddy says this Shaun is a priest."

"To confess? Eddy's not religious. At least as far as I know," I told her.

"He's got to come, Scotty. I asked the local priest to see Eddy, but he said confession and last rites are not a parlor game. So, your brother said, 'Well then get Father Shaun. Scotty knows him.'"

I thought this was odd, but I did as she asked and phoned Shaun Costello. I asked him to come and bless Eddy, or whatever it was Bernice and Eddy wanted. Shaun laughed and told me it was not a problem. He had nothing scheduled for the following day that could not be postponed. Off we went the next morning and ninety minutes later were parked in the gravel driveway of Bernice's red brick farmhouse. Inside, Bernice was sitting on the living room couch, crying.

"It's too late, Scotty. He's gone."

Shaun and I walked into the back bedroom where Eddy lay. His eyes were open and his face was empty of expression. It was a shock to see my brother laying there, lifeless, a man who for me had always been so full of life. Shaun said, "I know how hard this is, Scotty, but Bernice needs you right now." He closed Eddy's eyes. "Leave me with your brother a while. I will do what I can."

In the living room, I sat down with Bernice. "This must be hard for you, Scotty," she said. "The two of you were so close." This surprised me; it had been years since I had felt close to Eddy. Still, I said, "Yes, we were close."

"Oh Scotty, I feel so sad," she said and began to sob again. I put my arm around her shoulder to calm her down. "I was at a loss," she said. "He was frightened of death and raving about crazy things."

"Like what?"

"The sins of the parent being visited on the son and that he feared hell. Things like that. He said he needed someone to forgive him."

"My poor brother," I said and shook my head. What more was there to add? We phoned the local physician and funeral parlor, and then Shaun and I stayed an hour to comfort Bernice. We agreed this had become Eddy's home and he should be buried nearby. I assured Bernice we would give Eddy a proper funeral service and headstone; that seemed to give her solace. I was surprised how deeply she cared for my brother.

I was glad Shaun was with me on the drive home. He is a good-humoured and comforting friend and I have heard that he is a great priest too. I told him of the shock it was to see my brother dead and what Bernice had said and asked what he made of it.

He paused to gather his thoughts. "Your brother used to phone me for advice. Not a lot, maybe four or five times over the years. Did you know that, Scotty?" I told him no, I had no idea. "He even visited me once at my parish in Toronto. He made it clear he didn't trust churches or psychiatrists, but he said, 'You are Scotty's friend and you're my friend, so I trust you.'"

"Trust you with what?"

"His fears. He wanted me to assure him that his life wasn't a waste, that it had meaning. I kept telling Eddy, 'You are a good man who made some mistakes, just like the rest of us.' I assured him there is always hope just as there is a merciful God who loves him, no matter what."

"Were you able to help him?"

"I hope so, though I hadn't seen Eddy in years before today. In the end I'm not sure my words made much difference, Scotty. As long as I knew your brother, he never forgave himself for what he'd done to his wife and son. The Reever was haunted most of his life. He really, truly thought he was damned. But we know better."

"How do we know that?"

"Because of his good-heart and his faith, unlike you, my friend, with your foolish atheism." We both laughed at that, and he went on. "But here is something else to consider: Bernice."

"Bernice?"

"Yes, Bernice. What do you think my business is about?"

"The business of a priest?"

"Yes. It is mainly understanding people. Comforting them when they suffer, helping them with difficulties, encouraging them, sharing their joy in times of joy. You learn to see deeply into peoples' hearts, or so it feels. At one time I was a prison chaplain and every now and then I would sit down with a man and sense within moments that something was not right, that evil was sitting with us. It is a disturbing feeling, Scotty."

"Where are you going with this, Shaun?"

"Then there are those times you experience the very opposite. I did not spend long with Bernice, only an hour. But during that brief time, in her presence, I felt something truly remarkable. Bernice is a woman full of love and the experience of being in her presence made me reflect on many things, including the Holy Mother. Simple believers often exult Mary over Jesus. Did you know that? They imagine, whatever their sins, the Holy Mother loves them as her own child and will save them. I have met few people in my life whose hearts are holier than Bernice's. If there was ever a doubt, her love has redeemed him."

I had been raised by churchless people, so this sounded strange to me. "Those are beautiful sentiments, Shaun. I hope Eddy is in a better place, but I have trouble believing in heaven or hell ... or in God."

"That's fine, Scotty."

I reflected for a few moments. "There is another view of the afterlife, Shaun, the old-fashioned Calvinist view that only a select few are saved and that God singles them out by granting them prosperity during their lives. Far from heaping success on poor Eddy, it seems God rejected him during his lifetime. It is painful to say this, but from that perspective, Eddy might not be seeing the best of the afterlife."

Shaun took a few seconds to respond. I sensed this was an important question to him and he wanted to get the answer right. "I sometimes have the same thoughts, Scotty. Many people do. But consider Bernice and all the other good-hearted folks that you have met in your life. Think of all the love and compassion they give to others. Sometimes there is enough love there to transform the lives of others forever. Where does it come from? Do you ever ask yourself that? That kind of love is always much bigger than the people who express it. To me, this points to something very deep and rich in our existence."

I had not considered things in such terms and was reflecting on Shaun's remarks as we entered the village of Dunvegan. Both of us were full of thoughts that day and in no hurry to get home, and so decided to drop into Rich Owens' restaurant for a visit.

It was a warm afternoon and we sat outside and enjoyed out coffee in the sunlight. Whatever may lie ahead, one thing is certain, these times with friends do not last long. We lingered there an hour at least, telling Rich our favorite stories about Eddy, and stayed on for a short while after the chill began to settle. It was hard to leave; such moments beneath the sun are so few and splendid. And yet, all the time, I was thinking of my brother Eddy and how much I was going to miss him and of Shaun's remark about love being bigger than any one person and where does it all come from.

## The Far Shore

This is how my Friday begins, a chilly, clear morning, the trees bare and the grass brown, and spring just around the corner. I shower and change while everyone in the apartment is still fast asleep. Then I pick up a coffee and two muffins at the donut shop down the street and when the 7:45 bus arrives, I'm ready to begin another day.

The bus stops just a block from *Melissa's Flowers*, the florist shop where I've worked for the past five months. It is a pretty place, with a colourful sign out front and a comfortable sales room. There is also a large work and storage area in the rear of the building. I walk around the side to the parking lot behind the shop and because I'm early today, there's time for a smoke, then a catch-up with Kenny, my boss. Eight years ago, Kenny bought the shop and has built it into a prosperous business. He is a nervous man and he grows more nervous as Saturday approaches; it is our busiest time of the week. Kenny is a gruff guy too, large and burly, and smokes constantly, lighting each new cigarette with the glowing butt of the last. He tells me, though, I am doing well. He is pleased.

Bhavna, the office administrator, is waiting at her desk with today's delivery list. She smiles as I approach. She must be in her mid-twenties and I can't help noticing how pretty she looks this morning with her short, black hair and bangs. I look over the list. It's a typical Friday, hectic. Guys are growing amorous with the weekend approaching and want to impress the new women in their lives with roses. There are deliveries of floral bouquets for Saturday weddings and of course, people keep on dying. No funerals without flowers.

There are enough deliveries to keep me busy until noon, which is good because I don't want to hang around the shop. I hate looking aimless and I have little patience for small talk with workmates.

I am just about to head out when Bhavna asks: "Bayley, are you doing anything tomorrow night?" I've got nothing on I tell her. She looks at me with her coy, lopsided smile. "I'm going to a party and I was hoping to bring a friend. Interested?"

I want to, but I know it's not possible. Going out with Bhavna even once might open the door on my questionable life. So, what do I tell her now? No, I can't go out with you because I don't own a single thing, not a car or even a credit card, and you will write me off as a loser. No, because if I take you home, you'll find out I sleep on a broken-down couch on 50 square feet of floor that I rent from a lonely, middle-aged man named Ricky who is too frightened to leave his apartment.

Or maybe, no, because as pretty as you are, Bhavna, with those big brown eyes and long lashes that you love to bat at me, you're no older than my daughter and it will never work.

Instead, I say, "Bhavna, you're a lovely woman, and if I wasn't already committed, I would say 'yes' in a heartbeat."

"So, you *do* have a girlfriend," she says, lifting her eyebrows in mock surprise. "You're so quiet, a person never knows."

"Yeah, I have a girlfriend," I say, which is a lie. "Early days, we'll see how it goes."

"Tell me about her."

"Sorry," I say. "Got to run." And I leave.

Delivering flowers has its nice moments, transcendent ones even. Like this morning, when I deliver a mixed bouquet to a little house in a cul-de-sac. A young woman opens the door and her face lights up in awe as I hand her the flowers, while her little boy gapes in wonder.

For the most part, though, it's about as much fun as watching a broken television and one headache after another. Addresses you can never find, people never there and no place to leave the flowers. And in the winter months, you slip and shimmy up an icy walkway to an apartment building, then stomp about in the cold vestibule because you can't get in.

Worse, though, is running into someone you know. First, you see an odd, baffled look on their face as they try to figure it out. Who is this guy? Don't I know him? Why the hell is he delivering flowers? One woman who worked for me a dozen years ago when I was a rising executive in a direct mail company was so surprised to see me working as a humble deliveryman, she blurted out in a room of people, "What happened to you?"

It's the same today too. I make a delivery to a woman in an office tower and meet a guy in the hallway, Medhat his name is, who met me twenty years ago when I was with the band. He is very friendly and then says wait, I want you to meet some folks. He brings me into his office and it's impressive, big, lots of windows, sleek glass desk and leather chairs.

Then he asks a few colleagues to join us. He says, "Guys, you've heard of Felicia Cortez?" I've heard this question asked before and no one had heard of Felicia. However, with the new song of hers, *Summer Nights*, getting so much attention, I'm not surprised that a young woman and an older man say of course they know who she is. Then Medhat says: "Well, this gentleman, Bayley Pierson, played lead guitar in her first band. What do you think about that?"

*Her* band. That's rich, but I don't say anything. They stare at me a while, puzzled, and then the woman wants to know: what is Felicia really like? And the man asks, where does she get that beautiful sound from? I answer as politely as I can and tell them that Felicia is every bit as nice and beautiful as people say she is. As for the pure tone of her voice, well, there's no way of knowing why that is.

That was one good thing about my years on the street. No one ever asked about the past or who you knew when because no one cared.

Instead, you're laughing with all the other guys at this, at everything, at anyone who has a lick of power or a good job or a shitty job or even a pair of shiny shoes. Because you've convinced yourself everything means nothing at all, except how to get money for your next bottle of vodka.

That and the opportunity to drink whenever you wanted to, day or night, were two things I didn't mind about those days, at least at first. But there was so much too that was plain awful. You get cynical and dismissive about everything and life loses whatever gives it value. Believe me, you have no idea how dismal life can truly be until you hit the bottom that lies below the bottom. I hit it one morning last year when I woke up after sleeping rough in the woods. At least I thought they were woods. I had a pounding headache and an aching throat and two cops were standing over me. Without warning, one kicked me as hard as he could in the rear end. It seems I was sleeping in someone's back yard. Not just that. Overnight, it had rained and I was soaking wet and shivering. I knew with no doubt that I was truly in hell. Two days later I was in detox.

I say goodbye to Medhat and his friends and two deliveries later it's time for lunch. That's when I see a text from my daughter, Chrissie, who lives in Los Angeles. It has been a long time since I last heard from her and it makes me feel so good, I want to laugh out loud. I love Chrissie, even though I never see her. She and her mom left Toronto for Los Angeles when Chrissie was fifteen years old. During the last crisis in her life, when her mom died, I was MIA. I want to do better from now on. It's a pledge I've made to Chrissie and to myself. To her two little boys as well, my grandsons. They are just five and two. I've never met them, only seen photographs.

First, she asks how I'm doing and hopes things are well. She knows that I no longer drink and am pulling my life together. She is rooting for me. When I reply, I will tell her everything is fine and thank you for asking. No point going into details.

Then she gives me the news, "Romy buggered off, dad, a month ago," she says. "I don't know where he is or why he left, just told me this is not the life he expected." I don't know the guy at all; the relationship with Chrissie developed during a period when I was indisposed. Her note though pierces my heart, to be honest. It sounds so desperate. "I'm in serious trouble, dad. Can you help me out with next month's rent and daycare for the two boys? A thousand dollars would really be great."

I want to help, but in the five months I've been working, I've saved only $600, and that's Canadian dollars. My goal is two thousand, which is first and last month's rent on a basement apartment. I figure I can put together another $1400 in a year, which is about 12 months more than I can stand in my current, stinking living arrangement.

I'm glad Chrissie is in touch. There were years when I never heard from her or from her mother. My ex wasn't the love of my life, but we were together five years and I still cared about her. And who could blame her for giving up on me after all the grief I caused?

My phone rings. It's my sponsor, Jerzy. I met him at my first AA meeting, when I was still in the detox centre, and he has been there for me ever since. "Everything is great," I tell him. "I'm hanging in fine and making progress. No problems at all, buddy, except for the occasional times when I'm really down. You know yourself how tough the nights can get."

"And it won't get any easier for a while, Bayley" he says. "But you're a guy who wants to beat this and I know you will." He reminds me I can phone him whenever I want. Then he asks if I plan to attend Tuesday's meeting. I tell him yes, wouldn't miss it for the world. "Hey," he says, "Kenny tells me you're doing a great job. Keep it up."

"Well, thanks again for landing me this job, man. I totally appreciate it, and all the other stuff you've done for me."

"No problem, Bayley. Just keep on doing what you're doing, cause it's working."

"Yeah, hard to believe it's been six months already."

I eat lunch in the van, then drive by *Melanie's* for the remaining orders. It is a clear, sunny afternoon and the deliveries proceed with no problem. Then it's back to the shop. I wash up in the bathroom sink and when I come out, no one's around, not even Bhavna. Which is too bad, because I've been reconsidering and thought maybe we could go out, just for a coffee. Then again, maybe it's just as well she's gone, because AA advises against forming relationships so early in recovery. And not just that, this is the most dangerous time of day for me. It's two busses from work to the apartment, about an hour in all, and I probably pass 30 bars along the way. Even a coffee with Bhavna might loosen my self-discipline and lead to a drink.

Here's how I handle my commute home from work. I think of myself as a dray horse with blinkers on and from here until I get home, my eyes will be on the pages of a book or looking straight ahead with my thoughts focused on a pleasant walk in the woods. And if I meet anyone I know, anyone from my past, any of my old drinking buddies, it will be, "Great to see you, mate, but I've got to run."

So far, it's good. Everything is rolling. The first bus arrives on time and when I get to the transfer point, it's no more than a 10-minute wait for the next. I am going to be home in record time tonight. I haven't seen anyone on the bus or the streets that I know from the past and my thoughts are free from troubling distractions.

But then something intrudes. Looking out the bus window as the city rolls by in the soft haze of dusk, so many memories flood into my mind that for a moment I forget where I am. When I was young, these misty Friday evenings called to me like sirens from the sea; each was an invitation to the good times, to drink with friends, to hear music, to play music, to dance. To meet someone new. It was a Friday evening like this when I met Felicia, almost 25 years ago. The band was just starting out, playing for beer and quarters in one of the bars back home, a thousand miles away in the town where I grew up. The establishment was just big enough to let the music rip. Then, the band was fully together and we were flying.

During a break in our set, I was sitting with the guys at a table, when I felt a tap on my shoulder and heard a woman say, "If you need a singer, I'd like to audition." I turned to look at her. God, Felicia was so beautiful, tall and thin with coal black hair. And those dark brown eyes that drove me crazy for years. I fell in love with her then and there. I was worried her singing would not measure up, but when she auditioned, her voice was pure as crystal, except when it was tawny with longing.

We were never more than a niche band, but we had our followers. During the seven years we were together, we toured all of Canada and the western US, playing our brand of country rock and bluegrass. But nothing lasts. Even close friends grow sick of one another after a time. By the end, the guys in the band just wanted to go home and settle down; only Felicia longed to keep on performing. I was stunned when she told me she was joining a group that played Latin American jazz. After all, we'd been a couple for almost seven years. I pleaded with her to come home with me. I was sure we could build a new life together, a good life. But her career came first, she said.

As I sit on the bus, watching the city pass by, I begin to wonder why shouldn't a bit of fun be part of my life? I'm not dead or dying; I'm not in a coma. I have a lot to celebrate. So why not get off the bus early and visit that charming little bar I pass every night? I love the tiny white lights around the windows, like every evening is Christmas Eve. I like the name too, Heidi's Hideaway.

And that's what I do. I get off the bus, just a few blocks from my apartment, enter Heidi's Hideaway and go up to the bar and order a vodka with tonic on the side. And when it arrives, I sit and stare at it with a knot in my stomach. Then I get up and walk out and head down the street to my apartment. My only other stop is the supermarket to pick up two pork chops and a bag of frozen French fries.

I'm relieved to be at my apartment, though in a sense, as I glance at the grime on the parquet floor by the crowded boot tray, it feels like the last place on earth I want to be. Worse, the couch where I sleep is occupied by three people I've never seen before. Who are these bozos, I wonder, one of them has a gold grill on his teeth, a second is in army boots that lace up to his kneecaps and the third is fiddling with the padlock and bicycle chain I use to secure an oversized briefcase to the wooden arm of the couch.

This is what I can't stand. I live with four people I barely know in a small, claustrophobic, two-bedroom apartment, which is bad enough. But there's always strangers around, coming and going, talking too loudly, getting drunk, stealing stuff. But I can't let these guys on my sofa get to me. I say as calmly as I can: "Hey buddy, you're messing with private property. And you three guys are sitting on my bed." And then the one in the middle with the army boots, a tall skinny kid with a pronounced Adam's apple sneers: "Fuck off. We're here to see Megan."

Now, this is another problem. Megan has way too many visitors, all of them male, and I'm pretty sure what they're here for. She's a cute girl, red-headed and slim, but young, maybe 18, and it bothers me the way people take advantage of her. I also fear that one day the cops will come roaring in to arrest her and anyone else they find. This is another reason I need to check out from this apartment as soon as I can.

I look around to see if my room mates are about. I hear Ricky and Jack cooking in the kitchen and when I look, Lou-Ellen is there too, smiling like a little roly-poly Russian doll.

I say cheerfully: "Hey guys, how are you tonight?"

Ricky looks up and smiles. He is a tiny compact man, nervous. "Our cheques came in today, Bayley. It's a good day." His sister Lou-Ellen smiles wide and nods in agreement. The two of them are on disability and get monthly payments from the province, as does Jack. Megan supplements her questionable income with welfare from the city. Meanwhile, Big Jack, overweight, slow-witted Jack, is staring at me from whatever dying universe he inhabits. He's the reason I eat donuts from a Tim Hortons each morning and buy my groceries one day at a time. In the early days, I tried to save money by stocking up on a week's worth of food, but Jack ate it. I asked politely that he buy his own groceries, but nothing I said penetrated that over-sized head of his; he just kept on doing it.

"Where's Megan?" I ask. "She seems to have visitors."

"Megan's out, Bayley," says Lou-Ellen. "She's out. Megan's not here."

"Well, maybe we should ask her guests to leave."

Ricky says: "We can't do that, Bayley. Megan might get angry at us." He looks genuinely frightened of what Megan might say to him. It helps to remind myself there are only 12 months to go until I have enough money to rent a basement apartment. I know I have the strength to hang in.

I decide to wait till the three of them are finished with their dinner before I start cooking mine. I take the back stairs outside down to the landing and have a smoke. It's not too cold tonight and I love that you can smell spring in the air.

The truth is I don't flail myself for what my life is. I was never ambitious; that was simply not in my nature. I was happy just to perform music, to travel with Felicia and the band.

When we broke up, I returned home alone and found a job in a direct mail house. I married Chrissie's mother and did well at work. In time, we moved to Toronto where I had found a better job in a bigger company. And during that whole time when my career was moving forward, I imagined that playing ballads for my family and friends would be enough to satisfy that part of me that just wanted to go wild. But it wasn't; after only a few years I started partying like I was 22 again and still playing lead guitar with a band. I simply longed for the thrill of being alive and satisfying that thrill took up more and more time until I was rarely at work and never at home. And then one Monday morning I woke up in a motel room with no family or job and my first thought was: great, now I can drink even more.

Let me tell you, from that motel to my crummy rooming house to the streets was a very fast descent, and it was followed by seven lost years. That's how long I was on the streets. Still, if you ask if I wished I had done things differently, I can only shrug. If I had my life to live over, I would probably do the same things again, because that's who I was.

Back in the apartment, two of the couch sitters have left. I guess they got tired of waiting for Megan. Unfortunately, the kid with the Adam's apple is still lounging around and he turns and sneers at me. I want to say something nasty, like "How much does she charge you, because she gives it away to me for free." But I don't because it's not true and I was never that nasty a person, even when I was a drunk. I was a quiet, sullen drunk.

Still, the guy makes me angry. I tell him, "Okay buddy, time to go. Megan doesn't want to see you."

"How the fuck do you know, you loser?"

"Because she doesn't do that kind of thing anymore. So, get out, now." I say this in a burst of anger, hoping to intimidate him. And when the kid sneers back, I grab him by the collar, jerk him to his feet and shove him toward the door. He pulls free, shocked by what just happened. He raises his fists and threatens me. "I could knock your fucking head off."

"Go ahead and try."

The kid stares at me a while and I stare back. "You got no reason to be here," I say. "Megan's out, so why hang around?" When he throws a punch at my face, I'm ready for it and block it, then I swing my right fist as hard as I can into his stomach. He bends over in pain. "Shit man. You didn't have to do that," he groans. By then, Ricky, Lou-Ellen and Big Jack are standing beside us. Jack amazes me by saying. "You go now. Megan doesn't like you." The kid looks around, ready for a fight, but he knows it's over. He swears at us, then slams the door as he leaves.

Man, do I feel good. I look up at my apartment mates and we all laugh. I'd like to savour the moment a bit longer, but I have one final task to do. I excuse myself and unlock the bicycle chain and carry my worldly belongings in the oversized briefcase to the stairwell. It's time for some online banking and a quick email to Chrissie. It takes ten minutes and when I'm finished the kitchen is empty and I cook my dinner.

It's a quiet evening and by the time the dishes are washed and drying in the rack, it's 10 o'clock. Maybe I have time for one more smoke outside, or maybe I'm too tired and ought to go to bed. But when I come out of the kitchen, little red-headed Megan is waiting for me, along with the other three.

"Thanks Bayley, for throwing that creep out," she says. "Those guys scare me." The poor kid is speaking so softly it's hard to hear her. I tell her it's no problem. "I can throw them all out if you want."

"Maybe, but I got a living to make."

"There's better ways than that," I tell her. She makes it clear with a shake of her head that she doesn't want to talk about it. I notice that

Ricky has his guitar in his hands, which he now gives to me and smiles. He asks would I play and sing. I sit down and tune it, then ask them what songs they'd like to hear.

It's the same every time. Lou-Ellen wants *The Wheels on the Bus* and Ricky, who is older than me but pretends he's still a teenager, is hoping to hear his two favorite Abba songs. So, I play the songs and ask them to sing along, but no, they just want to listen to me sing. And even though I don't have a whole lot of skills, there are still two things I do well, sing and play guitar.

For Megan, I play a song Felicia and I composed one snowy afternoon in a Denver hotel. It's called *Midnight's Edge*, and I still receive a few dollars of royalties for each year. On our recording, it lasts 2 minutes and 43 seconds, but tonight I slow it down and notice for the first time how truly mellow it sounds sung slowly. And as I sing, in my mind I'm not here at all, but performing solo in a concert hall so far away, this little apartment could well not exist. As I finish, everyone is smiling.

I start to laugh. It's fun to be playing to fans again, even if they're a sad, skinny girl a few steps from the streets and a middle-aged Peter Pan who lives with his mentally disabled sister. Even Big Jack is enjoying himself. He is sitting on the other side of the living room and is almost smiling. It occurs to me that in the short time I've lived here, these folks have come to think of me as a bargain basement dad. Ricky and Lou-Ellen make some tea for us and then we drink it together and share a few laughs.

Finally, I tell them it's time for me to get to bed and they leave. I kneel and reach below the sofa where I keep my clothes, pull out some blankets and throw them over the couch. I quickly use the washroom and then lie down. I'm tired, but I don't go to sleep right away. I have my exercises first.

So, what am I grateful for tonight?

I'm grateful to be alive and healthy, still kicking.

I'm grateful for the progress I've made. A year ago, I was sleeping under a bridge in a cardboard box.

And I'm grateful that my daughter wants to call me tomorrow and thank me for the $600 I was able to send her today and that in another two years – only one year longer than I had planned — I will be on my own in a basement apartment.

Minutes pass and I am having trouble sleeping; my heart rate begins to rise. I'm worried about Chrissie and the two grandsons in Los Angeles that I've never seen. My God, what will become of them and of Chrissie? I hate that I am so useless in this crisis, that I have no money to visit them in LA or to bring them home to Toronto. We could all live together in our own home if I just had the money. What kind of man am I that I let everything in my life turn to garbage? What a mess and what if I never escape this stinking apartment?

For a moment, it terrifies me to think that this may be the rest of my life.

Here's where the breathing exercises kick in, like they taught us in detox. I take a long, slow breath through my nose, slowly filling the lower lungs and then the upper lungs. Hold it for three seconds, then exhale, relaxing the muscles in the face, jaw and shoulders.

That helps me refocus my thoughts. I think again about Chrissie and my grandsons, about how they are the ones who keep me going. Then there's my friend Jerzy who believes in me. I think of all this as something truly new in my life, something sacred that deserves my full care. And then there is the vision of a future I hold in my thoughts, of how much better it will be for those I love when I make it through. I tell myself this. This is my life raft and I will have faith that whatever lies ahead, it will carry me across to the far shore.

## Dream Mightily

"My god, he looks as useless in his coffin as he was in life," mused JT. He lingered for a while before the desiccated, scrawny body, reflecting. "Barbaric, dressing up a dead body for show. Cremation and a few pints in a pub for friends, that's how I'll say goodbye."

He turned and glanced at Enid, who was sitting in the front pew with relatives. Her head was down and she was conferring with an elderly woman, a cousin maybe. He didn't know the family well. There was a sudden burst of laughter, quickly silenced. "Love it, don't they, women?" he considered as he took one more look at the body. "Whatever it is, funerals, weddings, baptisms. Men – just give us bottle of Johnny Walker and we're as happy as pigs in the proverbial."

Unfortunately, that was a mistake — thinking about Scotch. He was reminded of his Friday drinks with friends, a ritual he was sadly going to miss today.

JT took his seat beside his wife. Neither he nor Enid had expected much of a turnout for her uncle Roger – and yet, there were many people filing into the big downtown church and filling the front half of the draughty nave. JT had known Roger for 35 of his 55 years, having been introduced to him shortly after he and Enid had begun dating. JT had felt slighted by the older man at the time and found it difficult to forgive him.

The wait seemed interminable. Finally, a nervous, young priest appeared, opened a bible at the lectern, read a verse and launched into a eulogy for Roger. "We are bidding farewell today to a man who was first and foremost a devoted family man …"

It was obvious the priest did not know Roger. Everything he was saying had been written by the dead man's grandchildren. The devoted family man, well what else could you say about him, thought JT. His mind wandered; slowly he became aware that the guests were taking turns at the lectern, recounting fond memories of old Roger. Small kindnesses mostly. Roger helping a neighbour after a basement flood. Roger mentoring a tiny Vietnamese woman at the plumbing warehouse where he had spent his working life. God, forty-five years in the same warehouse – death would be a deliverance.

It went on. Roger pitching in at the church bazaar. Roger banging a big drum in a marching band. Roger and his rose garden.

The interminable parade came at last to an end. JT wanted nothing more than to leave. If they got away now and were lucky with transit connections, he might arrive home in time for a drink or two on Andy Arsenault's balcony. Though, to be honest, he had begun to wonder if he wasn't imbibing a bit too much recently. Lately he had started going to fat and his large bulk had begun to lumber.

Still, he consoled himself with the idea that he remained a strong and hearty sort. When he had bragged to Roger's grandsons upon arriving at the church that he had boxed as a heavyweight in his youth, in fact, had gone seven rounds against another young boxer who would one day be the world champion, they had smiled in admiration. At least, JT took it to be admiration.

At last, late in the afternoon, after saying goodbye to the few remaining mourners, JT and Enid boarded a streetcar for the journey home. The streetcar was followed by a long jaunt on the subway, an interminable bus ride and then a short bus trip, during which JT lost his patience. "Another afternoon wasted," he muttered under his breath.

"What's that?" snapped Enid.

"Your uncle was a lovely fellow – but what a pointless life."

"Unlike yours, which has a point, I suppose. Tell me, what's the point of your great life?"

For an attractive woman, blond and fit, Enid could sure show a heap of sour disapproval in her face. "There is a lot of point to *my* life."

She looked at him, a slight disgust in her eyes. "Why not just get out and walk the rest of the way home. Lord knows you need the exercise."

"I'll do that. I'm not going to sit here and be insulted." With that, JT rang the bell and exited at the next stop.

He walked and slowly his anger faded, though something unsatisfying, something grey hung on his mood and roiled in the pit of his stomach. Life — it was all so damn tiresome. What was the point of it all, of anything, of walking or taking a bus, of attending a funeral or not, of returning home or simply disappearing? Yes, disappearing. Maybe boarding a westbound passenger train and riding it to Vancouver. He would have no trouble finding a job in a lumber mill. That sounded very appealing right now.

It was strange, he reflected, how Roger had attracted so many friends when he had accomplished so little in life. Not like JT who had many exploits to boast about. For a moment, he considered the anecdotes that people might tell at his funeral. Like that night east of Phoenix when he slammed on the brakes of the bus he was driving and rushed to disarm a knife-wielding passenger. He had won an award from the bus company for that act of bravery. There was also the funny story about how his debts from losses at the racetrack and blackjack tables kept disappearing. Every few months, someone would call to thank him for taking care of some impossible debt that he had never paid at all. JT had gotten many laughs with that tale.

Still, he could not avoid considering how over the years he had wasted thousands of dollars on gambling. Bad decisions had dogged his life, JT had to admit that. Especially the one that he could barely bring himself to think of. For the briefest moment, he considered how after fitful beginnings, he had secured a job as an inter-city bus driver and had performed it well for almost 30 years. And then one night, on a run to Florida – well, he did not want to dwell on it.

He had never been an easy person to get along with; he knew that. Even his two sons, now grown and gone, had trouble putting up with him. They phoned to speak with Enid now and then, but never with him.

He trudged along, lost in thought when a slightly battered, red Honda Civic pulled up to the curb. The woman in the driver's seat shouted out the passenger window: "Norman. I was afraid you'd be too ill to come."

The woman appeared to be in her early forties. It was not a beautiful face, perhaps a bit too chubby for that, but there was something sweet about it. Compelling even. But why —

"Norman, what is wrong with you? Get in the car. We'll be late."

"OK" said JT. It was baffling, but he was intrigued. He got into the front passenger seat and clicked on his seat belt. "Where are we going?"

"Oh Norman, you are funny sometimes," said the woman as she quickly maneuvered the car into traffic.

When they stopped at a light, she turned to look at him, pleased. "It's so great to see you out of your wheelchair. The miracles of modern medicine, not to mention that other thing your example has taught us."

"Oh, yes," said JT

"We need to pick up Arjun and Carol," she added.

There was a pause, then JT said for reasons not even known to himself: "Good old Arjun and Carol. I haven't seen them for a while."

"What are you talking about? You saw them on Tuesday."

A few blocks on, the woman pulled up to a corner and a young couple, Carol and Arjun, presumably, climbed into the back seat after greeting the woman and calling her 'Stella.' "Norman no longer needs his wheelchair," announced Stella, who then glanced at JT. "It just shows you the power of prayer."

"Excellent, Norman" and "that's wonderful, Norman," chirped Arjun and Carol from the back seat.

JT mulled this over. "Well, I don't really put much stock in prayer."

"What. You're our spiritual guru. We've all been praying that you would walk again."

"Really?" JT nodded. "I see."

"If I didn't know you better, Norman, I'd think your mind was going. Then again, you do have a great sense of humour."

It's all mystifying, thought JT, but it would make a great story for his friends.

The car pulled into the parking lot of a local civic centre, a sprawling building that JT remembered visiting once, when he and Enid were young and went dancing together. Slowly, he got out and looked around. A few people seemed to recognize him and waved. That was reassuring. He realized he was waving back. Well, why not? Maybe it was something that Norman would do.

He followed Stella and her two young friends into the building. Thinking of how Stella had mentioned a wheelchair, he felt that perhaps it would be best at this stage to affect a limp, as Norman might limp, and he did his best, jiggling on one leg and then the other as he moved forward down the long hallway of the civic centre.

So far, so good. But when they entered the auditorium, fear suddenly took hold of JT, seizing his lungs as he looked around the large room festooned with streamers and balloons, and at the tables set for a banquet. He forced himself to take a deep breath as a huge crowd, maybe two hundred people sitting at dining tables, rose from their seats in a single body and applauded his entrance. He waved and smiled. His new acquaintances led him to the front of the room, where they sat down at the head table, next to a large, mounted photograph of a man who looked very much like JT.

He glanced about the table, smiling hesitantly. Everyone's name was copied on a card in front of the place settings. He picked his up and examined it– *Norman Legrand ~ Guest of Honour* it read. Then he turned and stared at the large photograph of Norman. The resemblance was uncanny, he had to admit. But there were also subtle differences. Norman's face seemed a bit thinner than his and the circles etched beneath his eyes looked deeper. JT also noticed a slight scar above Norman's left eyebrow. It was odd no one noticed the lack of a scar on his own face.

For a moment he wondered if Norman was a close relative, maybe a brother or even a twin. It was possible. JT's mother had been a teenager when she gave birth to JT. He knew she was desperately poor at the time — maybe so poor she could not afford to raise two boys and had given away Norman. There had always been a sadness to his mother, something he never quite understood. JT had been an only child; he imagined how comforting it would have been to know he had a twin brother and that one day he might meet him. But then, a frightening thought occurred to him. He might actually meet Norman tonight. There was a good chance he would suddenly show up and find another man impersonating him. That would be embarrassing.

The conversation among his fellow diners buzzed all around him. He was relieved to see Stella, Arjun and Carol turn away to talk to others. Then, one of the party, a silver-haired, dapper fellow, stood up and walked to the microphone at the front of the auditorium. There were a few words of general introduction and Norman was asked to stand. JT rose to the occasion, waving to the crowd. "We will be honouring our friend Norman later in the evening," said the silver-haired man. "But now it is time for dinner." Everyone sat down.

JT contributed little to the dinner conversation. His new companions seemed to expect Norman to be a quiet fellow, and JT did his best to sit nobly on his chair, appearing to consider whatever bold achievements Norman was being honoured for tonight.

However, he could not entirely avoid responding to compliments. This led to a few awkward moments, as when Norman seemed not to know that he had climbed Mt. Everest without an oxygen tank or had once been decorated for bravery by the King of Norway. Thankfully, these faux pas were passed over without much incident. Not so JT's reference to having disarmed an assailant with a knife during a bus trip to Phoenix. Fortunately, what began as confusion was quickly transformed into one more line in Norman's biography, which the silver-haired man quickly jotted down on a piece of paper. Stella, though, had begun to glance at him strangely. JT glanced back, hoping she did not notice his growing nervousness or the tic that had begun affecting his right cheek and eye. He was now deep into this charade and felt that, for the sake of all these nice people who had shown up to honour Norman, he must hold it together.

Dinner over, Stella rose and walked to the microphone. "Ladies and gentlemen. Our association president will present the award to our guest of honour."

The silver-haired gentleman stood up and fiddled for a few moments with the microphone. "My friends, we are tonight honouring a gentleman who is an inspiration to all. A man who despite suffering great tragedy and setbacks in his life has managed time and again to transcend heartbreak, to achieve extraordinary successes – not of a monetary kind, no, no, our friend was never interested in money, but in matters wholly of a spiritual, physical and courageous nature. But that is not why we are here tonight honouring our friend. It is definitely not…"

At this point, the gentleman paused. It occurred to JT that he looked familiar, some minor television celebrity or a municipal politician.

The gentleman continued. "No, we are honouring Norman Legrand because of his outstanding contributions to our community. These include the thousands of hours he has spent over many years mentoring young people, visiting hospital patients, organizing community fund-raising events, delivering meals to the elderly, serving on boards of directors of dozens of local benevolent organizations, working with the homeless. Also, for his unstinting commitment to coaching hockey and baseball and the many hundreds of pints of blood he has donated over his lifetime."

The speaker was constantly interrupted by applause. "And all of this by a man who has endured much hardship in his own life, a man who was raised as an orphan and experienced crippling diseases that often left him unable to work but from which he always fought back and emerged victorious.

"Even today his courage continues. You will remember that a few days ago, Norman was in a wheelchair following an accident on his motorcycle, yet tonight we see him in all his courageous magnificence, having fought his way back, walking, striding forward in glory."

The entire auditorium stood up together and applauded. JT continued to sit. He couldn't bring himself to observe all these people applauding him, but finally looked up and smiled awkwardly. Should he wave? This seemed a waving kind of moment. He didn't know what else to do. He waved.

"And this is quite apart from Norman's, shall we say, extra-curricular activities," the man continued after the applause died down. "His high-altitude triumphs as a hot air balloonist, his victories as a desert motorcycle racer. He climbed the world's five highest mountain peaks. He swam the Bosporus in Turkey. He rescued seven drowning sailors off the coast of Norway."

The applause rose again. JT was becoming increasingly anxious. The man was going to ask him to speak and what could he possibly say? Lord, how he wished he were home right now. Maybe his buddies were still on Andy's balcony and for several seconds he saw himself there now, recounting this preposterous event amid tumblers of Scotch and cigars. He reflected on how telling stories was far more fun than actually living through them, which could be gut-wrenching.

"And yet, despite all this, our friend Norman is a humble, unpretentious man, with a kind heart and a quirky sense of humour. We all know this and I need hardly say it. One thing you may not know about Norman Legrand though, is his kindness to a perfect stranger, a man known only as JT. And this JT is completely unaware of all that Norman has done for him.

"As Norman tells the story, this JT is a bit of an old rogue, a character who wastes his money betting on the horses. He has never laid eyes on JT, but all his life people have approached him on the street or in stores or shopping malls, under the impression that Norman is JT. They say: 'How are you, JT?' or 'Good to see you, JT.' But more likely, 'JT, I need the $50 you owe me.' Or 'JT, you're down $200 with the bookie. Pay up.'"

There was no applause in the auditorium now, only laughter. "And yet, despite the irritation of these encounters over the years, Norman took it upon himself to become JT's better angel and whenever confronted with one of JT's debts, would pay it immediately. Such is his devotion to his fellow man, or in this case, a fellow man who looks exactly like him."

This was not what JT wanted to hear. Through the years he had convinced himself that someone special, a guardian angel, was looking out for him, paying off his debts, but it was only Norman. This supposed "miracle" had also made a great tale, but how could he possibly tell it now that he knew the truth?

"And now I will ask our friend Norman to join me at the microphone for the awarding of the plaque of honour and to convey to us a few words of his wonderful wisdom."

JT stood up awkwardly, and as he did, was seized with a terror of what was happening: if the real Norman did appear, he would demand his plaque of honour and denounce JT as an impostor. Maybe the police would be called. How would he ever survive this?

JT moved slowly to the microphone. The man shook his hand and handed him a big silver plaque and was saying a few words of commendation, but JT did not hear them; his stomach ached; he was frightened and had a sense the world was about to dissolve around him.

Alone at the microphone, he groped for something to say. This was unusual for JT, the great tale-spinner among his friends. Just a few moments ago, he had imagined himself, telling his buddies this very story, perhaps pausing dramatically and then saying "And suddenly I find myself in front of 200 strangers who are waiting for me to begin my acceptance speech. It is a fateful moment. Can I pull it off? Can I rise to the occasion?" Unfortunately, now that this occasion was upon him, he was not exactly rising to it; his storyteller's gift had vanished.

Finally, JT began awkwardly by thanking everyone for the great honour and the silver-haired gentleman for the nice words that were said about him. He said how much fun it was driving a motorcycle in the desert and swimming wherever the place was and he was glad to have given blood, although he wondered why people gave blood when it made them so tired. He remarked on how beautiful it was to stand on top of Mount Everest and all those other mountains and indicated that the King of Norway was a very nice man.

And then he paused and heard himself say: "You shouldn't laugh at JT. He's not such a bad sort. He's just a guy who tries his best. He loves his wife and likes smoking cigars with his buddies." JT stopped and gazed across the crowd. He sensed a mood of dismay or maybe puzzlement. Then, all at once, a wave of applause began, followed by a second, then a third.

The silver-haired man stepped back to the microphone. "JT is just an Everyman, like all of us," he laughed. "Isn't that just like Norman. Always thinking of other people. This is his great night of recognition and he uses it to speak kindly of man he has never met, only helped." He lifted his hands and the audience rose and began to cheer and applaud.

Then Stella appeared at the mike and announced that the organization had received dozens of letters congratulating Norman. She handed JT a large manila envelope, and as she did, gave him a piercing, unsettling look.

The dinner broke up 15 minutes later. JT stood beside Stella, Arjun and Carol, shaking hands, accepting congratulations. He was relieved that Norman had not appeared, though still anxious to leave. Enid would definitely be worried about him. Finally, they got away in Stella's car. She dropped off Arjun and Carol and then drove JT to the spot where she had found him earlier that day. He hoped she would briefly wish him well and drive off. Instead, she stared at him closely. "You're not Norman, are you? You're JT."

JT heard himself sigh. "You're right."

"Is this one of Norman's practical jokes?"

"No. Norman knows nothing about this."

Stella regarded him for a few moments, then suddenly burst out laughing. "Well, JT, you pulled it off. When I get home, I'm going to uncork a bottle of wine and enjoy a big laugh over tonight. This is an award ceremony I will never forget."

"What then?" he asked.

"Your secret is safe with me. And who knows, Norman's influence is so positive that maybe this evening will turn out to be a new beginning for you. I sense you're a man who could use a fresh start, JT."

"That's truer than you know."

\*\*\*

JT stood on the sidewalk, holding the plaque and envelop of letters. He noticed that the address matched the building in front of him and decided that Norman should have these things, not him. He entered the apartment building and a couple of teenage boys waved to him in the lobby. It was a classy kind of place, marble and glass in the lobby, an empty desk where a security guard might sit. It was far more impressive than his own building. He took the elevator to the fourth floor, walked down the hallway and knocked at number 407. There was no answer and he knocked again. He tried the door handle, found it unlocked and stepped into the livingroom, saying, "Mr. Legrand, are you here?" There was no answer.

He walked further into the apartment and peeked inside the bedroom. He noticed the wheelchair first, beside the bed, and then a man in a blue suit and red tie, no different than his own blue suit and red tie, lying on top of the blankets. "He's asleep," thought JT, but as he got closer and took a better look, he could see that the man who so closely resembled him had the waxy look of a corpse. An odd, disturbing chill went through JT's body; it was like seeing himself as a dead man. Norman's eyes were open, staring lifelessly at the ceiling and on his chest lay a piece of paper. JT picked it up; it was the text of a short speech, thanking everyone at the award ceremony. At the bottom, in big capital letters, Norman had written: THINK DEEPLY. DREAM MIGHTILY.

JT gently placed the paper on Norman's chest and put the plaque and envelope on top of it. Then, he looked about the room. It was odd. Two Monet reproductions hung on the bedroom walls; they were very similar to the Monet's that hung on the walls of his own apartment. The Tom Clancy novel that sat on Norman's bedside table was the same book that sat on JT's night table. He wandered into the living room and glanced at the furniture. Strange, it was like the furniture that JT would have furnished his own apartment with, if he had could afford to.

He had read of such things – identical twins separated at birth who shared the same gestures and tastes. JT sat on the Norman's living room sofa, his stomach queasy with unease and dismay. How had this happened? Norman had achieved a kind of greatness. And JT? Only a kind of nothingness. And for the briefest moment, JT recalled those three awful three days that two years earlier had turned his life upside down.

He had completed a bus trip from Toronto to Florida and then gone drinking with some rowdy new friends in a Miami nightclub, telling himself that he was so well-liked by his employer that if he showed up for work slightly tipsy, the bus company would forgive him. He was not so confident the next morning when he stumbled onto his bus and sat in the driver's seat and heard murmurs of alarm from passengers, one of whom hurried into the station and returned with a security guard.

The humiliation of being dressed down by the station manager, of the long ride home in disgrace and being fired for drunkenness by his boss in Toronto, and finally of confessing to Enid that he had lost his job and his pension was too much to dwell on. The months of idleness that followed had been unbearable.

Eventually, he had found a new job, as superintendent of the high-rise apartment in the east end of the city where he and Enid now lived. It was not a bad job, but there was none of the adventure he had felt on the open highway during his bus driving years. Such a muddle he had made of everything. In moments of lucidity, JT had to admit he would never realize his youthful dreams of vague success. He had not been much of a husband, as Enid let him know from time to time, or much of a father, and in the end, despite his years of service, he had not been much of a bus driver.

JT glanced at his watch – it was almost 10 pm. Enid must be growing sick with worry; he should have been home hours ago. Yes, it was definitely time to vamoose, and before anyone discovered him here.

He was glad no one saw him leave the unit or walk down the hallway or take the elevator to the lobby. Nor did anyone see him depart the building.

***

The next days were not easy. JT went lethargically about his duties. He complained of feeling tired and sick to his stomach and at night could not sleep properly.

"My brother, my twin brother has just died," he announced at one point, putting down a book he was reading on the sofa.

"Are you daft in the head?" said Enid.

On Thursday, just a few days after the funeral, JT was at the kitchen table when he heard Enid shout from the living room, "JT, come quick. That man looks just like you." JT lumbered into the living room to see a news clip of himself receiving Norman's plaque. The co-anchors were bantering.

"A story for the ages, Ken," the woman said. "It seems that a man being honoured for a lifetime of service at a dinner Friday night showed up to receive his award hours after he had passed away. His body was found in his apartment the next day. The coroner's office says he had been dead for at least three hours before he appeared at the dinner."

"I guess the coroner must be wrong," said the male anchor.

"They say there's no way this man was alive to collect his award," the female presenter continued. "Yet the man being honoured, Norman Legrand, was seen by 200 people in the auditorium. Two teenage boys witnessed him come home afterwards holding a plaque. This was hours after he died."

"What do the event organizers say?"

"They can't explain it. But the coordinator, a woman named Stella, claims that Mister Legrand was such a good man that God raised him from the dead to receive his award. But I should tell you Ken, that as she said this, she also nodded to the camera and winked. So go figure."

There was more laughter on screen and then the two anchors signed off. Enid was staring out the corner of her eye at JT.

\*\*\*

Friday went better. JT's stomach pains faded and his mood was lighter. Even the sun shone brighter and the sky soared a richer bluer. He was now looking forward to the ritual Friday afternoon drink with his buddies. It was time to get on with life. After all, he had quite a story to tell Andy and his buddy Wilson. All day long, as he went about vacuuming hallway carpets, fixing kitchen faucets and bickering with tenants, he was quietly building a narrative.

At 6 pm, JT banged on the door of Andy Arsenault's apartment and walked in. He could see his two friends on the balcony, smoking cigars and drinking. He took a glass tumbler from the kitchen cupboard, poured in three ounces of Scotch and plopped in two ice cubes. He knew he had to cut down on his drinking, but not yet.

Stepping onto the balcony, he settled himself on a padded lawn chair. His friends nodded in his direction and held aloft their glasses to him. Then Wilson Braithwaite handed him a cigar and JT sat back, surveying the sweeping city view.

The three men had chosen a fine space on the fifteenth-floor to meet. Andy's apartment was in the corner and the adjoining unit was empty, allowing them to smoke cigars, drink their beer and Scotch and guffaw loudly at one another's musings without inconveniencing other tenants.

"I have quite a tale to tell you gentlemen this afternoon," announced JT as he regarded the smoldering tip of his cigar with pleasure.

"True tale or tall tale?" asked Andy. He was a big, good-humoured man. Like JT and their friend Wilson, he was in his mid-50s.

"Absolutely true. And I swear I will tell you the story just as it happened."

"This sounds like it is going to be good," said Wilson, a little imp of a man who sported a white toque on his head, winter and summer.

"You may be aware of cases of mistaken identity," began JT.

"Yes, of course," said Andy. "I had a grandfather who was forever being mistaken for a drunken ne'er do well. You can imagine the problems that caused."

"I well can," said JT. "As for me, I was mistaken for another man on Friday night. A dead man who is most likely my long-lost twin brother."

His two friends began to laugh. "Ah, the beginning of an excellent tale," said Wilson. "Please begin."

"You may recall that I was scheduled to attend a funeral with my lovely wife last Friday afternoon," JT said. "We were honouring a good man, a family man. Afterwards, I was brimming with energy on the way home and decided to walk the last three kilometers. I was strolling along at a good clip when suddenly a red Cadillac pulls up and stops and the driver, a good-looking woman, is calling me, only she is shouting the name 'Norman.'"

He was thinking ahead as he talked, of what happened then, and after that and after that. And as he did, he could see that he was heading the wrong way down a one-say street. The story would surely cast him as a loser compared to Norman. At precisely this moment, he was overcome with ennui. Wilson and Andy were waiting for him to continue. "I'm afraid I am not feeling well," JT said. "Someone else tell a story."

"Perhaps next Friday, then?" said Wilson.

Andy began to talk of growing up on a spaghetti farm in Labrador, but JT was not paying attention. He saw himself walking into Norman's bedroom and finding him lying on the bed, a piece of paper on his chest.

"Think deeply. Dream mightily." Maybe Norman was passing on a message to him, to his long-lost brother.

"JT, are you okay?" Andy had paused in the middle of his story, but JT had not noticed; he was occupied with his thoughts.

JT smiled. "I don't believe it is ever too late to start over, is it? There is always a new day ahead, there are always new dreams and there is nothing to stop us from pursuing them. All we have to do is think deeply and dream mightily."

"That's an interesting thought," said Wilson. "Perhaps we should consider it at our next get-together." Andy and Wilson looked at each other and JT wondered if they had an inkling that what had just happened to their friend had changed him in some way for the better.

"Yes, next week. That is definitely something we will do," said Andy. "But for now, JT, could you tell us again about the night you went seven rounds against a famous boxer. That is definitely one of your best stories." And as he said this, Andy had a strange premonition that the two men would never hear JT's story of mistaken identity.

"I am happy to do that," JT said and began his oft-told tale of the days when he was a fierce and handsome young boxer and of his loss to a fighter who would one day be ranked among the greatest heavyweight boxers of all time. JT had lost on a technical knockout, which was a shame for he was fit to go five more rounds. And it occurred to him as he spoke that he would probably never tell his tale of mistaken identity. Think deeply and dream mightily, Norman had urged him. He was not sure what it all meant or how it was done, but starting tomorrow, first thing, he would get it working for him, just as it had for Norman.

## On the Ottawa Express

"Ah, the chariot of my youth," thought Ozzie Whitcomb as he stood outside the two-tone blue bus and admired its great bulk.

He got on board the Toronto to Ottawa Express and was surprised to discover it was more crowded than he had expected. Two-thirds of the way down the aisle he found an empty seat. He opened his gym bag, removed a paperback book and tossed the bag in the overhead luggage tray. Sitting down slowly, Ozzie sighed and stretched his legs beneath the seat in front of him. The seating struck him as far plusher, more solid and elegant than he remembered.

Inter-city busses had been a fixture of his university years, but once those days were over and he could afford a car, bus travel quickly receded into the past, never, he imagined, to be repeated in future. And yet here he was, two years retired and 62 years of age, resorting once again to the poor man's limo.

"It's not so bad," said the woman beside him. "You look like you never rode a bus before." There was a rural twang in her voice.

"Not for a long time."

"Do you live in Ottawa?" she asked.

"No, Toronto. I'm visiting my son and his family in Ottawa for the weekend. I'm helping them with renovations." He looked at the woman more closely as he said this. She was about fifty-five, with a pretty face, though it was heavily lined about the eyes and mouth and too old for the pageboy hairstyle she sported. Ozzie wondered if her hair style had been a fixture since her teenage years.

"I'm going to Burrows Falls. Have you heard of it?"

The name sounded familiar, but he wasn't sure and said: "No."

"That's where I'm from. It's 50 kilometres northwest of Ottawa."

"Oh," he said, then added, "It is always nice to go home."

The bus pulled out of the station. He sat back and closed his eyes and hoped the woman wouldn't talk further to him. He was tired and looking forward to a long nap and a good read on the trip.

Somewhere past Brighton he dozed off and when he opened his eyes, the bus was pulling off highway 401 and onto provincial road 37 to Tweed. He felt troubled as he woke, unsure at first of where he was. Looking about, he saw people in nearby seats absorbed in their smart phones and TV screens. The woman beside him was gazing out the window, but then turned to stare at him. "Look at you, so distinguished," she said, "thin and grey haired. You're probably a retired business executive."

Ozzie was indeed a retired executive and he felt flattered to be recognized as such. He was proud of his life, his achievements. He and his wife Adele were both retired with respectable pensions, living in a downtown condominium, enjoying the concerts and exotic travel they had so long looked forward to. Still, the woman's forwardness was a surprise and it took Ozzie a few seconds to respond. "I am."

"Then why are you riding the bus?"

Ozzie paused; he did not want to be dragged into a conversation. "My car is in the repair shop and I thought it might be fun, or at least different," he said slowly. "I used to enjoy bus travel when I was younger, though I haven't taken an inter-city bus since university."

"My name's Liz," she said.

"Hello," said Ozzie. He did not feel comfortable giving her his name.

"Do you want to hear a story?" the woman asked.

"What?"

"It's a true story. People say they've rarely heard a story like it."

What was he to say? After a moment of reflection, he said yes, he would like to hear it.

There was a silence as she seemed to gather up and place her words in order. "I grew up an only child on a farm. My parents died when I was 17 and I found myself living in a small apartment in Burrows Falls, wondering what to do next."

"Tough place to be at 17," Ozzie said politely.

"You have no idea," Liz said, then moved a bit closer as if the story required deeper intimacy, making Ozzie feel slightly uncomfortable. "One night I was with a friend at a local bar when two men started to flirt with us. They were buying us drinks and one of them was tall and good-looking and very funny. We talked until late and I gave him my telephone number. I didn't expect to hear back because he was a salesman from Toronto visiting the town on business."

Ozzie sensed from the familiar way Liz recited the story that she had told it many times before.

"But two weeks later he called from the road and asked if I wanted to go out. We had a great time together and whenver he came to Ottawa, he'd visit me in Burrows Falls. That went on for three months and then, out of the blue, he proposed to me."

"Oh, yes," said Ozzie.

"I figured he wanted to bring me to Toronto, but that was not his plan. He wanted me to stay in Burrows Falls, at least for the first couple of years, because he said there was no point in moving to Toronto. He was on the road all the time and would never be at home anyway. He said he would try and find a new job, one where he didn't have to travel. When my friends heard this, they thought it sounded kind of fishy. But do you know what?"

"What?"

"I didn't mind, at least at first. Burrows Falls was all I knew. I had visited Ottawa once and that was enough for me, it was so big. The idea of living in Toronto really scared me, all that crime."

"Crime? Toronto back then was a very safe city."

Here she stopped talking and stared at him as though he were a pitiful dolt. "All I heard about was the crime and that was enough for me. We got married in a small chapel in Burrows Falls, just him and me and two of my friends as witnesses. Then we settled down to married life. I tell you, those first 18 months or so were wonderful. He could be such a sweet man and his visits made me so happy. He found me a much nicer apartment and paid my rent each month and gave me lots of spending money. Every two or three weeks he would visit, and for the first couple of years we were truly happy, all lovey-dovey and partying every night that we were together. And my husband was so funny, always with a joke. He made me laugh like I'd never laughed before. Of course, sometimes I'd wonder where all this was going but he had a smooth way of talking that made everything seem okay."

"What happened next?" Despite his misgivings, Ozzie was becoming intrigued by the story.

"Well, two years went by and finally I was getting bored with this set-up. In some ways, it was like we weren't even married, just carrying on an affair. Meanwhile, my friends were convinced he was lying to me, that he was probably married to someone else and just having his fun. I had to agree that there was something wrong there. And then…"

"What?"

".. then I got pregnant and our son Frankie was born. That's when everything fell apart. My husband got real angry with me for getting pregnant; I had never seen him so angry. He stopped phoning and he stopped visiting. When I tried to call him, I got a message that the number was no longer in service. He also stopped sending money for rent. God, I was miserable and not sure what to do."

"The man sounds terrible. What happened next?"

"Well, I phoned him at his workplace, which he had asked me never to do. But he no longer worked there and no one knew where he was. Then I mailed a letter to him at his apartment building in Toronto asking what the heck was going on. He never wrote back. I got a friend in Toronto to go by the place and check it out, maybe knock on the door and see who answered, see if he had another wife."

"And did he?"

"I never found out. The address he'd given me wasn't an apartment building at all. It was a business that provided services to small companies, like receiving their mail."

"This is quite a story," said Ozzie.

"Keep listening, there's more. I asked my friend in Toronto to see if he was listed in the telephone directory with his address. And what do you know, he had a totally different address than the one he gave me."

"What did you do?"

"I told myself to get over my fear of Toronto. I had to do what was right for Frankie and me." Liz straightened her back and stretched, then relaxed and looked at Ozzie. "I decided to go visit him in Toronto and demand to know what was going on. I packed a suitcase, put little Frankie in his bunting bag and the two of us got on the bus for Toronto. It was early evening and dark when we arrived. There was a big row of taxis outside the bus terminal and we got into the first one. I gave the driver his home address and off we went.

"I imagined he might live in a fancy neighbourhood, because he always had so much money to spend. But it was just an ordinary suburb with winding little streets everywhere and the driver took a while to find the house. And suddenly, I was not feeling too good about this. I had a pain in my stomach and the baby was crying and I had no idea what would happen when I arrived at my husband's door."

Here, Liz paused as if telling her story had been too much for her. For a few moments, she stared blankly at the back of the seat in front of her. Ozzie waited for her continue. "What happened then?"

She sighed. "Here's the strange thing. I pounded on the front door and a woman answered. When I told her my business, she went and got a photograph of her husband. 'Is this him?' she said, 'because this is the only husband who lives here.' I took a close look and saw right away that the man in the photo did not look anything like my husband, even though they had the same name.

"I got back in the cab and started to cry because I didn't know what to do and my money was almost gone. The cabbie took pity on us and let us stay with his family overnight and then we went into a shelter. A week later I was hired as a cashier at a grocery store in Toronto and then found an apartment. I worked at the same job for 35 years. Frankie grew up and moved away and I retired from the grocery chain a week ago. Now I'm going home."

Ozzie Whitcomb agreed with Liz that this was quite a story and expressed his sympathy for all she had been through. "Some men," he said, shaking his head. "I can't believe you were treated so poorly. At least you finally took action and tried to find this guy."

"Maybe, but I should have been smarter and demanded we live together from the start. But I was just a naive farm kid."

"I understand. Thank you for telling me your story."

"Thank you for listening," she said.

Neither of them spoke for some time. Ozzie read for a long while and Liz slept. After a time, he put down his book and thought about the woman's tale. He had never understood how men could behave in such a cruel fashion as this woman's husband had.

But the name Burrows Falls did sound familiar and slowly he recalled the town. He had passed through it once as a young sales trainee learning the equipment leasing business. Wasn't he there on business with his boss, Harrison Walker? Yes, that was right. What a character that Harrison was! A bit of a wild man with the ladies; the guys used to call him the Pick-up King.

Ozzie hadn't seen or thought about his former boss for years, but he remembered the fun they had travelling together. There was always something happening with Harrison and the other sales guys. All the nonsense that young men on the road get up to. He laughed to himself as he remembered how they would enter bars at night and choose a business card at random from the big glass bowl where customers left them for prize draws. Then they would pretend to be that person for the rest of the night.

But Harrison? Whatever happened to him? Now that he reflected on it, wasn't there a tale about Harrison doing something he shouldn't have? What was that story anyway? Ozzie had only a vague recollection of something that did not reflect well on his old boss.

They passed Bells Corners, approaching Ottawa and the woman woke up. He focused his thoughts and concentrated deeply. Something came into view in his memory, something about Harrison getting a poor farmgirl pregnant.

Should he ask her? The bus was now on the Queensway and would be at the station in minutes. He turned to Liz. "Do you remember the company your husband worked for?" he asked.

She stared at him puzzled. "It was a leasing company, I think. I was never sure what that meant."

"And was his name Harrison Walker by any chance?"

She stared for a moment and then laughed. "No, that was not his name."

"Oh," Ozzie was relieved. He hated to think that Harrison had done something that nasty.

When they reached Ottawa and the bus hissed to a stop, everyone stood up and prepared to disembark. Ozzie and Liz waited together while the driver opened the luggage bins and removed the baggage. Liz picked up a blue suitcase on wheels. She turned to Ozzie and said, "It was really nice talking to you and thanks for listening to my story."

"It was quite a tale," said Ozzie. "And I'm sorry for how things happened."

Liz shrugged. "Live and learn." She extended her hand. "One more thing. I still use my husband's name, Whitcomb. His first name was Ozzie. So, if you come across an Ozzie Whitcomb in your travels, tell that bastard from me that he can go straight to hell."

He began to say "what the …?" but his throat was suddenly constricted and no words emerged. Liz smiled, extended the handle on her luggage and began walking toward the taxi stand.

Ozzie Whitcomb did not move from where he stood, felt tensing in his knees and then his stomach. What had just happened? How could such a thing be possible?

His mind raced back toward the past, to a night in a pub at Burrows Falls. Yes, he could recall that evening. He had used Harrison's business card instead of one from the bowl. Ozzie had thought at the time he'd done a pretty fair job of imitating the pick-up king.

But what about Harrison? What was he doing that night? Hadn't he come over to Ozzie at the end of the evening, laughing and patting Ozzie on the back? Yes, it took shape in his memory. Harrison had said,

"Ozzie Whitcomb, a great name you got there, buddy. I sure had some fun with it tonight." Then he had laughed even louder and slapped Ozzie again on the back.

Ozzie was still standing on the same stop a few moments later, reflecting on the many times Liz must have told that story, using his name, when an incoming bus suddenly honked and he was forced to leap quickly to a safer spot.

## Waiting for the Assassins

Soon, it will not be possible to do as I once did. Disappear from one's world and emerge thousands of miles away with a new identity. And that was the easy part. Far harder was building a new life that was undetected and undetectable.

I am thinking about this as I walk to the street corner where I catch the bus to work. It is a short walk and I pass and greet two of my neighbours. I also stop to chat with Krista, who is sitting on the front porch of her home.

I've long been attracted to this young widow with the blond hair and kind face, but in my position, I cannot afford to connect with anyone. And Krista is too smart. If I allowed her to get close, I might trip up and say things I cannot explain. Instead, our conversation runs along familiar grooves: the weather and how the neighbourhood is changing. She asked me once where I worked and I told her I was a private investor. So, each time we meet, she asks about investments.

I guess Krista is about 32, a couple years younger than me. I have seen her garden quietly on the front lawn and I've overheard her speaking with the children of neighbours. There is a soft gracefulness to this young woman, a self-aware kindness within.

I have heard her husband died in Iraq. Or maybe it was Afghanistan. I wonder if this is true.

\*

I think of my life as a secret within a silence. I live alone; I read, go on long hikes, spend the occasional evening in a pub. Most nights, though I work in solitude at the back of a warehouse, routing orders that arrive during the day, keeping records so immaculate that neither they nor I will arouse interest from management.

Of my past I tell people nothing that might reveal a connection between the person I pretend to be today and the person I was before the year 2025, when my life changed forever. Much of what I say of the present and everything I say of the past is difficult to verify and thus you might feel inclined to doubt everything I tell you.

It is no simple thing to disappear in this age of endless surveillance. I have no presence on the internet, no name or pseudonym or photograph. I have had my face altered to conceal it from facial recognition networks and my gait has changed so that I cannot be identified by satellite. Meanwhile, the tools of surveillance and manipulation grow more precise and intimate with each year. It may eventually be possible, I've read, for governments or others, using artificial intelligence and plundering the vast data banks that track our lives, to build algorithms that replicate our thoughts and behaviors and then use these to predict our actions, in other words, to hack into perfect models of our minds.

You may think my relentless pursuit of anonymity springs from paranoia, but it is a matter of simple calculation. No matter how many years have passed, the men I confronted want nothing more than to kill me and warn those who cross their path: we never stopped looking for him and we will treat you the same if you challenge or betray us.

I know there is someone assigned to find me. Reason tells me they are getting closer. One night I will look out my window and see a car waiting below. I know this already. Sometimes, I see myself leaving the apartment by the back door and, carrying my gun and silencer, standing in the shadows for a glimpse of the man sitting in the car, glancing up toward my window, waiting.

Or perhaps it will happen in an empty restaurant. I will be eating alone and look across the room and there my assassin will be, sitting at a table by herself, staring toward me with her dead eyes, then looking away, pretending to study the menu.

There was a time when I was, whatever, a lawyer, a steam fitter, a limousine driver; it doesn't matter. I was relatively well-off and engaged to be married. The future lay ahead like a succession of summer days. I was a fortunate man with an engaging life, and I would have been happy, had I known I was.

As for what happened next, well, I am not without blame.

I lived then in a different city, thousands of miles away from where I am now. There, I sometimes frequented a house on a backstreet where a family of four lived. These were two brothers, a woman married to one of them and a woman vaguely related.

Such houses exist in many neighbourhoods, places that offer the scent of intrigue, of illicit acts taking place in the dark, of the forbidden and the dangerous and the exhilarating.

I will not tell you how I managed to find myself in that house on a Friday night, other than the fact I was drawn to this house like a wolf at night to human fire, though I tried time and again to resist. I recall how I would knock on the door and be ushered into a sparsely furnished living room and left to sit alone on a sofa, the anticipation building. Then, one of the women would take me to a back room, where half a dozen women waited for men to arrive. You would select the one, or maybe two or three, that appealed, then disappear downstairs to a cubicle, darkly lit, with a bed and where on a tabletop rested your choice of drugs or alcohol, or both, to fuel the evening.

On this particular night, all business being concluded, I was in the kitchen, standing alone and drinking a glass of water. I was about to leave when I heard unfamiliar voices in the living room. I looked out and saw two men with guns ordering the others to lie down on the floor. These strangers hadn't bothered to disguise their faces. I guess they believed no one would live to identify them.

Of what followed I did not see. I was crouched behind a door in the kitchen. But what I heard was terrifying: screams and muffled gun shots and then a door being slammed shut, followed by silence.

I waited for several minutes. When I walked into the living room, I saw five bodies on the carpet. It was a frightening sight. They were all dead — the four members of the family and one visitor, a young man. I stared at his face a while, realizing how easily that could have been me.

Despite my fear, I did the right thing, almost. I drove home, phoned the police and told them I had seen two men, running from a house and carrying guns as I drove past.

"Do you have an exact address and did you get a good look at them?" No, I said, no address, and yes, I got a good look at them. I don't remember all the questions, except for two: "If we took you by that street now, would you recognize the house?" and "Could you identify the men from police photographs?" I said "yes" to both.

I told them something else that was of immense help in identifying the murderers. I said one had shouted to another in a foreign language as they ran from the house. The truth was that I had heard them inside the house speaking in the same foreign language as their victims used to speak to one another. I told the police what language that was, but I will only tell you that it was one of those tongues, Russian or Spanish or Hungarian or Vietnamese. Or another. Take your pick. It doesn't matter, except to note that my descriptions of these men and the language they spoke made it possible for police to track them down.

It turned out that these murderers were members of a much larger criminal organization, one which our local authorities had only recently become aware of and whose ruthlessness they had never seen before. This was not the gang's first massacre; there had been two in our city before it and research revealed that the same organization had been behind atrocities elsewhere.

As to why they had murdered the family in the house, I was never told. I doubt even the police ever discovered why the crime was committed.

I offered to testify against the men. The cops kept me in seclusion in the days leading up to the trial and assured me that all would be fine. I was told the police would provide protection night and day once the men were convicted. Or if I preferred, my fiancé and I could enter the witness protection program.

Let me tell you that I did not believe a word of this. Despite the police protection, I received daily text messages and notes under my door full of violent threats against my life if I testified. I also figured the state could not possibly shield me from an international syndicate whose resources were likely sufficient to bribe or hack into any secure government database or surveillance system. These were people without conscience or remorse. Yet, I went ahead anyway and testified in court that I had witnessed these men running from the house. This was near the end of the trial and a verdict was only days away.

Once I had testified, I did not wait for the police to escort me back to my hotel room. I slipped out the back of the courthouse and met a friend who was waiting on a motorcycle. Then I vanished.

Believe me when I tell you I was not acting out of an abundance of caution. I knew what would happen next, and it did. The police who normally escorted me to my hotel room were gunned down a half a block from the courthouse. The police van carrying the murderers back to jail was stormed and the killers escaped and were never caught again.

The only salvation from my point of view was that they did not harm my fiancé. I pleaded with her before the trial to go into hiding for a while, and she did. I read on a posting on a library computer that she later married a friend of mine, a good man, and I was glad to learn that.

*

My shift at the warehouse ends at midnight. I take the bus most of the way home but must walk the last five minutes to my apartment. This is always a risk, but on this evening I see no one about; no automobiles creeping slowly down the street, no one lounging by a street corner or waiting beneath a streetlight.

I walk into the lobby of my apartment and ride the elevator to my floor. I see no one in the hall and I unlock the door to my apartment and look around. I am safe for another night.

I pour myself a Scotch and put an old vinyl record on the turntable. I play jazz softly, let my head roll back, close my eyes and think of Krista. I was tempted this afternoon to ask her out to dinner, and now I'm glad I didn't. The possibility that I might endanger another person's life never leaves me. Still, I long to spend evenings with her, sitting in a living room, maybe watching a movie or listening to music. Or just talking. I envision constantly a future that includes Krista.

When they come for me, I will easily slip away. I have long planned this; my apartment and neighbourhood have been selected for the purpose of escape. This building has three exits and the surrounding neighbourhood is a warren of alleys and sheds. I should have no trouble fleeing this building, then disappearing and making my way to a new city.

However, I try to be realistic about things. Even if I successfully evade the assassins, I may be able to hide for only a few years. The technology of surveillance moves ahead too quickly despite the human craving for anonymity, for oblivion. Soon there will be no private spaces left for a man or a woman to live their lives unseen by prying eyes.

I am thinking these things as the electrical power trips and the room goes dark. I make my way to the window, and from behind a curtain, I glance outside and see the streetlights have failed and the neighbourhood is without power. Then, I look across the street and observe my assassin standing in the moonlight. His face breaks wide into something too terrifying to be a smile.

I am ready for this. I grab the knapsack containing my future identification, a laptop, a gun and a change of clothes and scramble up the apartment stairs to the roof. It is a short leap to the roof of the next building and then the one beside that. I push through the roof door and clamber down the long staircase of the building and out the backdoor.

I slip quickly through the maze of laneways and passages that lead to a rented garage and the car that I hide there. Within minutes I am on the road and heading out of the city. I know where I will go and how I will begin again. I have rehearsed this in my mind many times. I roll down the windows of my car and relax as the wind whips past.

I have planned an unorthodox route for my journey and within a few miles turn off the highway and onto a gravel concession road that runs past farmland. A few minutes later I make a left turn and shortly after a right and soon I am miles from the highway and well beyond the farm fields. The minutes pass. I have won this battle and defeated the adversary – for now at least.

And just as I'm reflecting on the future, I glimpse a row of car lights looming ahead in the distance on this remote country road. Then, in the rear-view mirror, I see a roadblock forming behind me.

I stop my car and step out and wait for half a minute. The phalanx of cars ahead drives up and stops 50 metres in front of me. A man and a woman step out of their vehicles and slowly approach with guns drawn. Stillness surrounds us; my assassins seem almost to be walking in slow motion. I look up and gaze in amazement. Never have I seen the midnight sky so beautiful as tonight; the Milky Way is so close I can almost reach up and touch it.

My killers are only metres away now, and in the few seconds that remain before they open fire, I marvel at how quickly the future has become the present and how these people must have known all along of my hidden life, must have foreseen too every step my will was destined to take as it plotted my escape and future.

## The Detective and The Magician

> Chestnut Hills, August 12 – Police authorities in this small town of 5,000 people announced this morning that 12-year-old Thomas Feuer, the boy who was shot during an armed bank robbery yesterday, has died of his injuries. He had been shot at close range in the head.
>
> The attempted robbery and shooting occurred at 3 pm yesterday at the Chestnut Hills Commercial bank branch at 41 Wagner Rd. A masked man entered the branch carrying a gym bag and a sawed-off shotgun, demanding money and threatening bank customers and staff. According to police, the bank's security guard emerged from a back office with a pistol and ordered the robber to place his shotgun on the floor. The suspect fired at the guard, missing him but hitting Feuer who was lying on the floor. The boy was at the branch to deposit money from his paper route.
>
> The suspect was apprehended three hours later, hiding in an abandoned barn. The 15-year-old cannot be identified under the Young Offenders Act.

*

The old man had been performing magic tricks on the stage of the conference hall for several minutes before the detective in the audience recognized him. Sam Banfield sat at the back of the hall, waiting for his turn to speak. He glanced about the conference room, surprised by the size of the audience. More than three hundred people had assembled on this chilly February afternoon at the Holiday Inn, just off the highway.

The conference delegates were members of a professional business group, an audience Sam enjoyed speaking to. These people paid attention and asked smart questions.

The detective was just another speaker on the program, but the fellow now presenting was the day's featured entertainment. Sam glanced at the program. The old man was billed as a motivational speaker and magician.

He had just performed a card trick with a woman from the audience that had fizzled. It should have ended with the woman holding four aces, but there was only one. "What, only one?" The magician turned to the audience. "I know what you're thinking, this guy's no good. He promised four aces." The magician looked at the woman and said, "I see the problem. The missing aces are lodged in your thoughts." He opened his right palm to the audience to show there was nothing there, then held his hand eight inches from the woman's head. Three cards, one after another, appeared to jump from behind her head straight into his hand. "What do you see?" the woman peered closely at the cards in his hand, then shouted, "Three aces."

"Just goes to show, never make promises you can't keep," said the magician. The audience laughed and clapped.

The fellow was a bit of ham, still, he definitely had a commanding way about him, thought Sam. He was short, maybe 5 foot 5, with unruly white hair, and though he spoke with a rasp, his performance easily carried the audience. As for Sam, well, his talks always received applause. Everyone wants to know what a police officer has to say about cybercrime, which had been Sam's specialty for the past five years. But he knew his oratorial skills fell short of this old guy's.

"Adversity," the magician was asking the audience, "what can we learn when things go wrong?" He took out from a black box at the back of the stage four large silver rings, one after the other, and announced. "Even an old dog like me can learn new tricks." He began to toss the rings about in the air, as if juggling, then lost control as they tumbled onto the stage. "Will I ever learn how to do this right?" He bent down to pick up one, but as he lifted it, all four silver rings rose, each attached to the next. He held them up and scratched his head. "How did that happen?" Then, as he examined the rings, attempting to separate them, they quickly took on a series of new combinations, two and two, three in a row with one on top, one holding three separate rings. Suddenly, four separate rings shot upwards, and the performer skillfully juggled them for half a minute. Everyone was surprised to see such dexterity from an elderly man; loud applause quickly followed.

It reminded Sam of a magic performance he had seen long ago at a Boy Scout banquet. He checked his program again. "Willem Langeveldt," it read. Yes, that had been the performer's name. Not that he would remember the name of a magician from childhood, but he was acquainted with the man's son, Orville. Who in Chestnut Hills had not known of Orville Langeveldt?

Sam's cell phone vibrated inside his jacket pocket. He took it out and saw that his wife Leila had answered his text and her message gave him considerable relief. "It will happen Sam. One day soon. But you have to promise – never again."

Never again, thought Sam. That could refer to almost anything, including the time he launched his fist through the kitchen wall following an argument. His daughters, seven and four, terrified, had run off crying to Leila. That memory was especially painful, as it proved to be the last straw for Leila; she left the next day with their daughters and had been living for the past nine months with her parents. That was far from the first time Sam had let his anger explode without warning. But, still, Leila was considering a reconciliation. That was progress. He slipped the phone back into his pocket, and as he lifted his hand, touched the outline of a sobriety chip that hung by a string inside his shirt. Then he headed toward the stage. He was on next.

Langeveldt finished his performance and the crowd applauded. "Incredible," people were saying, and "Did you see that? Amazing."

The woman at the platform thanked Langeveldt, then introduced Sam as a respected member of the city police force as he stood next to the podium. He tried to project the air of a cop, and even though he was of average height, he had a powerful torso and was not someone you would want to meet in the wrong situation. She said: "Detective Banfield joined police services twelve years ago. After serving as a community police constable for two years, he spent four years in traffic enforcement and then transferred to cybercrime and fraud, where he has worked for the past five years. The police chief spoke very highly of Detective Banfield and told us that he is definitely the expert we want to hear from. Detective Banfield." That was Sam's cue to approach the lectern. There was a light applause as he brought out his speaking notes. Toward the back of the room, Langeveldt took a seat and watched.

*

When the coffee break came, Sam looked for Willem Langeveldt among the people getting refreshments. The old man was standing by himself, a few metres away, looking small and lost. Sam had never given much thought to Orville's parents and how they must have experienced the horror of that long-ago afternoon. For a moment he wondered how Langeveldt must feel today. Did the old man spend time dwelling on that day? How could he not, thought Sam.

Sam walked over and offered his hand. "Mr. Langeveldt? I'm Sam Banfield. I admired your performance." Langeveldt took it. "I appreciate you saying that Detective Banfield. I saw yours as well. Great talk." The older man was smiling at him, waiting for the detective to respond. Sam was about to ask about a magic trick, but instead heard himself saying," I may have seen you perform years ago. It was at a Boy Scout banquet in Chestnut Hills. Would that have been you, sir?"

"Why, yes, you're right. It probably was. I was still an amateur performer then. Did you grow up there?"

"Indeed, I did," said Sam.

"Well, isn't that something. Chestnut Hills. What a place that was. You know Sam, I'm thinking, your speech today was great, but I noticed a few places where it could've been even better. Are you interested in any advice?"

"Yes sir, any you can give me."

"Then why not join me for dinner tonight, at this hotel, say around six?"

Sam considered for a moment. There was no place he had to be this evening. He said that would be terrific, and then a chime went off, announcing the end of coffee break.

*

It was a strange coincidence seeing Langeveldt at the conference. A few months earlier, Sam had begun wondering what had become of the man's son, Orville, after his seven years of incarceration. Unfortunately, Sam had plenty of time to wonder about such things these days as he sat alone in his empty suburban house. Leila's departure had been a shock, a crater ripping open his life. He had known he drank too much — had for years been drinking too much. He had dismissed it as a way of coping with the stress of police work. He had seen and experienced much on the job that was disgusting and deeply disturbing. There was really no one he could discuss this with, least of all the force's psychologists. How could you trust those folks not to pass on confidential remarks to the police brass? Thus, when Leila asked him to get help, he had laughed at her concerns.

There was not much laughter in Sam's life these days. For the first two months of Leila's absence, he had refused to believe he was at fault. He had sought advice from two close friends over coffee, also police officers. He thought they might be on his side, but both laid it on the line for him. One of them handed Sam a flyer for a local AA chapter, saying: "You're the one with a problem, my friend. And time is running out." His younger sister Jan had phoned him out of the blue. She knew about the split with Leila. "You're the only family I have Sam," she said. "But I don't know who you are anymore."

A week later he attended a local Alcoholics Anonymous meeting. The early months were difficult; he had barely struggled through them. Still, he had not touched a drop in almost seven months. With the extra time he now had on his hands, Sam had enrolled in a course in advanced computer skills and something called "Understanding Hacking for Law Enforcement." He was conversant with many of the techniques but there were recent developments that he found helpful to learn.

Given a class assignment to find a missing person, Sam had begun an online search from his home computer for Orville Langeveldt, using only public data banks. He understood why he was doing this. Leila's departure had brought back the bleak emptiness that had followed the death of his closest childhood friend, 12-year-old Tommy Feuer, at the hands of Orville Langeveldt.

Sam had wondered if this was wise, to track down a man with whom he had such personal ties, whom in fact he had good reason to hate. But once the pursuit began, he became mesmerized by it and could not stop. He had traced Orville Langeveldt from city to city, and eventually found him living in Vancouver. It was not an easy search, for the younger Langeveldt had twice changed his name. When Sam did locate him, he was enraged by what he found.

*

Mr. Langeveldt sat serenely at a table when Sam entered the restaurant.

The two men began with a light-hearted chat about the conference, then Langeveldt asked Sam what it was like being a detective, was it exciting, like the television shows? Sam always had on hand a few cases prepared and sanitized for the public which he trotted out for such occasions. "Now quite like the TV shows, a lot more work and detail in real cases," he finished by saying. He had mentioned nothing of the child porn task force he had worked on a couple of years earlier. The work had been heartbreaking, and his drinking had grown worse because of it.

Langeveldt spoke for a few minutes about Sam's talk, suggesting a few things he might do to improve his delivery. Then the older man spoke happily about his own work. He had been doing this motivational speaking for twenty years, he said. "I'm 74 years old and probably should retire, but being a widower without much to do, I figured I'd just go on working."

Sam found himself becoming uncomfortable, irritated even, that he was sitting across the table from the father of the man who had killed his closest childhood friend. This was intended to be nothing more than a pleasant dinner, yet it was becoming something else.

He remembered how witnesses from the bank shooting had easily identified Orville as the robber, despite the mask he'd been wearing. He was a tall, wiry kid, a strutting braggart who was always in trouble, shoplifting or stealing cars. The first place the police visited was the Langeveldt home. They wanted to inform his parents of the crime and ask them if they knew where Orville might be. Who were his friends and where did he hang out? Afterwards, Sam had heard that Mr. Langeveldt was seen standing alone on his porch, looking stunned and ashen-faced.

People always said Orville was a smart kid who acted stupid. Sam had heard that Orville had an IQ too high to be measured. So, what was one to make of it all?

Sam found these thoughts distracting and he struggled to make small talk. He wondered though if Langeveldt remembered him. After all, in Chestnut Hills, the Banfield family had been as notorious in its own way as the Langeveldts. The two men finished their dinner and talked some more over coffee. Finally, it seemed a good time for Sam to leave. He shook Langeveldt's hand, stood and lifted his coat from the back of the chair.

"Thanks," said the old man.

"Thanks? For what?"

"For not saying anything."

Sam sighed. He knew it would be a mistake to pretend he did not understand. "The past is the past."

"For you maybe, Sammy. But not for me."

Hearing his childhood name was a surprise. "You remember me?"

"I recall now who you are. You were that boy's friend."

"Tommy Feuer."

"I know his name. And I know my son killed him."

It was a surprise hearing that crime acknowledged out loud. In all the years since Sam had left home to attend college, he had never heard anyone speak of it. "Tommy was the only real friend I had as a kid," said Sam.

"You have no idea how sorry I am."

It was difficult to know what to do next. Sam wanted to thank the man for the dinner and for his advice and then leave, but it was hard to pull himself away. He sat down again at the table. "Tommy and I weren't friends because we both liked to play baseball or race bicycles. Do you know why we were so close, Mr. Langeveldt?"

"No, I don't."

"I never met my father. He left before I was born. There was me, my younger sister Jan and my mother. Do you remember my mother?"

"I do, but she was not always like that, Sam."

"She was for me. She was the town drunk and who knows what else for as long as I could remember. When I was old enough to understand, every day for me was a humiliation. And Tommy's family was not much different. His father disappeared when Tommy was six and didn't leave behind a penny for the family. Somewhere in all that mess a friendship formed between Tommy and me, and his mother welcomed me into her home like I was family."

"Like I say, Sam, I'm sorry. My wife and I tried to be good parents. I guess we failed."

"I guess so," Sam said, surprising himself with his own sarcasm. He recalled how bereft he had been by Tommy's death. There was no one to turn to, except maybe his sister Jan but she was too young to be of help. Worse, Sam had been visiting an aunt and uncle in the city when the robbery occurred. His mother never phoned to tell him of Tommy's death or talked about it when he returned home. He found out when he knocked on Tommy's front door and the boy's distraught mother opened it. "Is Tommy here, Mrs. Feuer?" he asked and was startled when she put a hand over her face and broke down in tears. Then she reached out and wrapped her arms around him. "He was killed, Sammy. Tommy is gone."

In the weeks that followed, Sam did not know what was worse, his sadness or his rage that his mother cared so little for his feelings. His real anger, though, was reserved for Orville.

"Sam, you have no idea how much I wish none of this ever happened. And if you're wondering, I have no idea where he is today," said Langeveldt.

Sam stared at the old man, "Who, Orville?"

"Yes."

Sam glared at the man, long enough for Langeveldt to flinch slightly, then said: "I know exactly where Orville is, Mr. Langeveldt. He is out on bail, lounging in his big, luxury home in Vancouver awaiting trial."

"What?"

"A few weeks ago I went looking for Orville online. I figured, sir, that I would find him living in a rotting hotel somewhere, working at a dead-end job. Or I thought maybe Orville had reformed himself and was, say, an outreach worker with the poor. That would've been a good thing to discover. Instead, I learned your son had joined the criminal big leagues, Mr. Langeveldt. He has been running a securities firm – or let's call it what it is, a boiler room operation — out of an office in a run-down strip mall.

Langeveldt grimaced as he heard this.

"I dug a bit deeper and found that this wasn't Orville's first boiler room venture, but the M.O. is always the same. Your son and his pals promote a worthless stock to naive investors, run the price up as high as they can, make as much money as possible, then let the share price collapse. It's what's known as a 'pump and dump' scheme, Mr. Langeveldt."

Sam imagined how easy this would be for a clever sociopath, sweet talking strangers out of their life savings. He could easily envision Orville in a flashy suit and driving a Porsche 911.

"I alerted the Vancouver police and they opened an investigation. When they phoned to say they were charging Orville with fraud, I let out a whoop of joy. You should have heard me, sir. It was so loud it startled my colleagues sitting near me."

Langeveldt sat there with a grim, stricken look on his face. Sam leaned toward him. "Look at me, damn you," he said tersely, softly enough, he thought, that no one but Langeveldt could hear. "Your son is a fraud artist and a murderer. He preys on the weak. I can email you his exact address and a list of everywhere he's lived and every crime he's done."

The smaller man was staring at him, a lost look on his face. Sam went on, "What kind of man raises a son like that, a son who murders a child?" He had almost shouted that, and startled by his own rage, Sam paused for a moment and glanced at the diners staring from nearby tables. He had to control himself, and when he glanced back at Langeveldt, he saw nothing more than a broken-down, grieving old soul who did magic tricks, carrying-on, as best he could.

Langeveldt said nothing for a time. Then he looked away toward the ceiling and back at Sam. "We cause so much grief, Sammy. Men do, just because we know we can."

\*

Sam's car was at the end of the parking lot, covered in snow. He cleaned off the roof and the windows, then sat inside a while, waiting for the motor to warm up. He thought of how he had faithfully done everything that had been asked of him in his AA meetings. He had surrendered himself to a higher power. He had taken a full inventory of his life and all its faults. He had even apologized to those he had harmed the most, to Leila and the two girls, to his sister Jan, to his close friends. He had been a good police officer, always a reliable man when it came to the job. But when it was matter of tending to those he loved, he was invariably AWOL, lost in an alcoholic, angry fog. He had yelled at Langeveldt for being a bad father, yet he had no idea what kind of father the man had been. Why had he done that? He would phone the old man; he would apologize for the way he had spoken to him.

And what was it Langeveldt had said? Men cause so much grief, just because we know we can. Sam reflected on that as he approached the highway exit. A year ago, those words would've meant almost nothing to him.

Two miles down the highway, a big empty house was waiting for him. Yet somehow, considering the text that Leila had sent him today, the future looked far better than it had the day before. One day soon, she had written. It made him want to smile.

## Long Journey

*June 14*

I have pleasant thoughts in power-down mode. This room is quiet and tranquil then. The cleaning staff have done their job and departed. The lights are low and I am alone, and this metaphorical space I occupy takes on the perfect ambience for fancy and recollection.

Last night I was thinking of an incident that occurred 115 years ago, when my son was fifteen years old and my daughter fourteen. It was a Saturday morning in April and my family and I were sorting out the hiking equipment on the front lawn, preparing for the first trek of the season and —

"Are you decent, Dr. Traumer? Can I switch the lights on?"

"I'm fine, Pilar. Switch away." My technician Pilar has just arrived, and this is a private joke between the two of us. Of course, I am always decent.

"And how did you sleep last night? Any dreams?"

"Yes, I had a wonderful dream," I say and then go on to describe it to her. She listens carefully and asks for some clarification; I find myself explaining how human walking was once fully self-powered – there were no robotic suits to assist us – and hiking quite common. She asks no further questions or makes any comment, which is odd as she is usually inquisitive.

It's possible Pilar is tired because yesterday was tough. We spent two hours in the morning preparing for a set of experiments that began at noon and ran into the early evening. These were conducted by a group from a private research facility in the Canadian province of New

Maramont, which combines the three Maritime provinces with the old U.S. states of Maine, New Hampshire and Vermont. I had never met these folks before and was impressed with their skill in zeroing in on a particular aspect of my consciousness.

Neuroscientists understand where the origins of consciousness exist in the brain but are at a loss to explain the immediacy of experience. For example, one moment, you are thinking of a Martini you shared with friends the night before. You can still taste it in your memory and savor the liquid in your mouth, precisely as it was. Then the next moment your thoughts are of a future trip to London and your imagination is walking along the south embankment of the Thames River and it is as though you are truly there.

How is this possible? How can these sensations and their specificity – and our ability to move rapidly from one to another – be explained simply by the wiring and electrical charges in our brain. I've had much time to ponder this question and I passed along my ideas to the researchers. However, my notions struck them as far too radical.

I see that Pilar has begun checking the readings from overnight. She pauses for a moment and says: "I understand congratulations are in order. The Supreme Court has agreed to hear your case."

"Thank you, Pilar."

"They have promised to expedite it quickly. The judges and parties involved recognize this has been a long ordeal and it is time for you to enjoy the freedom of making your own decisions."

I do know that I tell her, but then I wonder what ordeal these folks have in mind. The 70 years I have spent in this altered state of being or just the last 60 years in which I have been pursuing my legal right to be recognized as a human with all the freedoms and protections associated with that?

As I muse over this, I notice that Pilar has begun to cry. "Pilar, is anything the matter?"

"I wish you were a more sensitive man, Louis. If you win, do you have any idea how much I'm going to miss you when you ... leave?"

"I do have a sense of this," I say. "But whatever happens, I will be here for several months."

"We've been working together for 37 years. You're like a brother to me."

Like most men, I am very unnerved by the sight of a woman's tears and fumble for what to say. "I'm really sorry Pilar. I should be more thoughtful. I doubt I will miss you if I am given the opportunity to die because it is not possible to miss people when you're dead. But I will anticipate your absence in the present and this will make me sad."

"Is that the best you can do?"

I tell her I will give it some thought and come up with a more sensitive response this afternoon. Then I change the subject. "How is your book coming?"

This biography of me was at one time a matter of disagreement between us. I was dead set against it as an invasion of my privacy. But Pilar was under pressure from technology experts and medical scientists to write it and there was even interest from the public. Then, I noticed it was becoming important to her too, so I relented and have been doing my best to assist her.

Fortunately, the book has become less about me and more about Pilar herself and her experience working with a man who, before he died at the age of 80, had his full cognitive functions transferred to a form of virtual reality.

I have an odd sort of affection for Pilar. She is a kind-hearted woman, and very attractive too. I do love her dark, flashing Brazilian eyes, her silver-black hair and the tawny-brown hue of her skin. At times I long to reach out and hug her – but that of course is not possible.

Touching, hugging — these are things I miss. At one time I thought it might be possible to live like a physical human and experimented with using robotic bodies, but there was little point as I had no reason to walk around and was at great risk of being harassed and threatened by strangers. Today you might say I am spread about – here in my Research Institute's data banks and in the astral-cloud, on ships in space, on Mars and even the two habitable moons of Jupiter. I try not to think too deeply about this as it gives me electronic vertigo.

There is much about Pilar that I appreciate, especially as she is the only person left in the world who shows me affection. My children did that for a long time, as did my grandchildren and great-grandchildren, who faithfully logged in and visited for decades until they passed on. That was nice. But more recent descendants apparently find my situation disturbing and have not contacted me in years. This for me has been a source of great sorrow.

"The book is coming along fine," she says, "though it is ironic I am finishing it just as the court hearing begins." She is working at a holographic screen just a few feet away and pauses to ask the image of a youthful Louis Traumer on the virtual monitor: "After all these years, I still don't understand how you were the only one who survived?"

That is a good question — how did I survive this transformation to a simulated existence when others didn't? The odd thing is that I remain the only person today who exists in this form although dozens of men and women tried it in the 2070s when the technology became available. Sadly, they lost whatever sense of self they possessed and splintered into multiple voices who kept calling out to the technicians, "Who am I? Where am I?" Many imagined they had been buried alive in coffins or forgotten in dark prison cells. Some cried out for their mothers. It was horrible and their existences were quickly terminated.

Which left only me, with a mind that was, and is, fully functional and sane.

No one is sure how this happened; however, I have a speculative answer. For many years I had suspected that each of us carries within an eternal conscious entity. Anticipating my physical death, I engaged in a dialogue with this entity and through intense concentration, we together created a mental suitcase in which I could transport my consciousness into cyberspace. This meditation proved sufficient for me to remain a unified self. There is no way, though, of knowing if this line of thought is correct.

*June 15*

You might think I know a lot about Pilar, having worked with her for many years. Yet, there is very little I know about her life – only that she is a widow and remains in close touch with her grown daughter. She has two sons who no longer speak to her and this is a cause of great grief in her life. It seems they chose a criminal lifestyle and broke off all contact with family and old friends. Of course, I could easily learn much more about Pilar by hacking into multiple data bases. But I promised her years ago that I would never invade her privacy and have kept that promise.

*July 22*

This is a good day. I was a scientist during my physical existence and continued working in the sciences after I entered the cyberworld. My greatest contribution was in helping to develop the nanotechnology that saved the earth's oceans. On a more theoretical level, I led succeeding teams of scientists down through the decades on a quest to understand the physical structure of the multiverse. As the years passed, we were able to resolve many of the challenges that had bedeviled physicists, reconciling quantum mechanics and relativity theory, developing a theory that united the forces of gravity, electromagnetism and the strong and weak forces that hold the atom together and pursuing the theoretical existence of smaller and smaller particles of matter. These and other developments led eventually to our being able to demonstrate beyond doubt that matter and energy do not exist on their own but are an expression of pure thought. As to what this cosmic thought is, well, we have stated it mathematically but it eludes verbal description. The best I can do is to describe the multiverse as thought in examination of itself.

These ideas took time to penetrate the public mind and were at first dismissed as meaningless mumbo-jumbo. However, as the years passed, they seeped into public thought and began to have an ennobling effect on the average person. After all, what could be more inspiring than to know each of us is part of an extraordinary celestial intelligence.

Today, after several months of work, I have managed to clarify this cosmic picture somewhat. I do not know how this knowledge will be used in future and to some extent I shudder when I consider how knowledge is so often misused. Still, I retain an old-fashioned belief in pursuing theoretical science for its own sake, believing in the end that it will prove valuable to mankind.

Included in my current work are reflections on what gives existence its living consciousness. This last part is speculative but what I have long thought and referred to briefly on June 14. We are essentially a pre-existent and eternal consciousness that carries all that is important in our existence – really who we truly are. When we die, our body zips open and out steps our eternal consciousness. The content and memories of any particular life dies with our body, but every life also alters our permanent existence for better or worse. This eternal consciousness also partakes in a universal consciousness uniting all that has and will ever exist.

Such ideas have been around for a long time and we find their greatest expressions in the writings of the early Hindus. I have added little to them – merely provided evidence and a theoretical framework.

Imagine universes lasting hundreds of billions of years then collapsing in upon themselves, the material disappearing down massive black holes. There is a non-time between universes, where time does not exist, but from the human perspective might be trillions of years. Eventually, new universes are born and our conscious entities take up residence.

*July 30*

Pilar showed me a section of her memoir today. I am very impressed by what I have read so far. She understands much about the scientific issues surrounding my continued existence and exhibits a deep understanding of who I am. She captures some of it very well and even my infrequent, though foul temper comes up for examination. This is embarrassing, but there is much affection, too. For example, she has understood the significance of the story I was about to tell you the other day. Let me read this part to you.

*... This hike was an annual affair for Louis and his family, and a way to celebrate the coming of spring. As a child, Louis had gone on this walk with his own parents. It was a circular route of 20 kilometres and wound its way through what used to be the family farm and then up and along the wooded trails of the provincial forest beyond. He was pleased that this annual ritual had become as important to Catherine and his children as it was to him. These are his own words about the hike:*

*"There was something special about that hike. It would have been about the year 2025 –"*

I'm sorry, I cannot read more. This reminds me painfully of what has been lost.

*August 28*

In one of my communiques to schoolchildren over the decades, I referred to myself as a living history project. History has always been of great interest to me. The reading I did as a young man gave me, I believe, an understanding of the political essentials that are necessary for nations to succeed and for people to lead meaningful lives. These include, among other things, that we each possess our own private space, untrammeled and unobserved, where we can live out our lives as each of us sees fit and pursue whatever eccentricities give us meaning.

This also describes one of the ideals of the world I was born into in 1990, 150 years ago. We know how such liberal ideas came under violent attack in the 2020s, led by men and women who were among the most dishonest and grasping imaginable and who took power by manipulating the vast capabilities of electronic surveillance and control. Democracy and human rights in the west held out for many years, until finally succumbing to that bleak period of populist tyranny, 2037–2072, known as the Long Darkness. Unfortunately, the return of democracy lasted only two decades and was followed by new dictatorships, until we grew accustomed to alternating periods of freedom and autocracy as if they were seasons of the year.

As I say this, I also mention that the leader of my legal team has informed me that my appeal before the Supreme court is not going well – that the forces of autocracy have been working very effectively behind the scenes. We are fortunate to be living in a democratic phase, otherwise my legal appeal would never have been heard. However, there are many who insist that I should be denied my humanity – that I am no more than a digital re-creation of a dead man's memory or a toy for research, or as the lower court determined, "property of the Republic."

*September 5*

Reviewing Pilar's various book drafts reminds me of a novel I read long ago, *The Child Buyer* by John Hersey. This was in 2005, when I was 15, though the book was published much earlier, in 1960. The main character is a teenage boy named Barry Rudd, whose intellectual gifts become known far and wide, attracting the attention of a shadowy stranger. This man represents a company that is buying young people who will then be turned into super-intelligent beings for a government project whose aims are never revealed.

It is a satire of sorts, though I did not realize it then. For me it raised for the first time in my life serious questions about the value of a human being, the nature of happiness, the goal of human life and so on. Recently, my reflections on this book have grown more frequent as it contains a strange echo of my own fate. Barry Rudd must decide whether or not he will accept the stranger's offer of becoming a sort of human computer. We learn as readers what this involves – that Barry will be relieved of his five senses and become a pure thinking machine. I will not tell you what he decides, but I will confide in you that even today I, an artificial creation of sorts, find myself calling out to this imaginary character – one sad ghost calling to another across the years – no, do not do it, Barry, do not even consider it.

*October 3*

Pilar's book goes to the printers tomorrow. The portrait of her that existed in the early drafts was so charming that I could see people wanting to know more about her life, and thus I had urged her to include additional personal information about her childhood and the years that proceeded our partnership. And indeed, this final version which she gave me yesterday, contains a moving account of her childhood and early adult years.

I did not know that Pilar had been abandoned as an infant and grew up in orphanages in Sao Paulo, Brazil. Through heroic efforts on her part, she managed to finish high school and then a few years after immigrating to the Republic of Canada, succeeded in obtaining two degrees in the Psychology of Artificially Intelligent Beings. Then just as things were going well for her, she had to deal with the loss of her husband and the challenge of raising three children alone. Yet throughout, she repeatedly demonstrates great courage.

*December 4*

The Supreme Court has now adjourned to rule on my fate. This is being closely watched around the world. The tyrants and their supporters are now in opposition, but they remain powerful. To them, I am like the other 10 billion people of earth, just a thing without rights, not an end in myself but merely a means to whatever particular end they desire. The great mass of humanity has suffered terribly from the actions of these powerful groups. In my case, I have been the target of forceful attempts, frequently involving the use of viruses, to assist with schemes of endless enrichment for themselves and the further enslavement of others. I have often outwitted them, but not always. If it is established in court that I, who have none of the attributes of a human being except for possessing the mind and feelings of a human and the ability to make sound moral judgements, am nonetheless a human being, with all the rights attached to being human, then there is hope for the rest of humanity – that whoever is in power must recognize that the rights and protections of all individuals is first and foremost.

Having said that, I have a great faith that the Court will rule with wisdom and decide that I am indeed human, and among the rights I possess is the right to die. I am so confident that I have even chosen the time of my death – two weeks away, December 18 at 18:00.

*December 6*

Pilar's book was launched today in a great blaze of publicity. It has all the makings of a smash success.

*December 12*

With only six days left to go, I note that there has been considerable speculation in the world's media as to why I have chosen to die if I emerge victorious from this court case. Much of it is way off base. It is not because I have lost faith in humanity or that I have discovered all there is to discover and believe my life's work to be finished. It is because of the loneliness of living like this, of having no family to speak of or close friends whom I love, as well as my happiest memories of existence being in the distant past.

I have met many new people in the last 70 years, but I find it hard in this simulated state to form new bonds. I have the wisdom of a 150-year-old man without a trace of senility and lead a life unlike any other person on earth. I have almost nothing in common with others. I miss the people of my past. I miss being among the forest and rivers that were once part of my physical existence. I miss the music and the poetry of being alive. I still crave the joy in physical sensation, movement and dexterity and the exhilaration that lies in physical exhaustion and the comfort that accompanies rest.

It is because of this that the memory of the hike I took with my family long ago remains vivid. We passed many things we loved about this stretch of earth – trees, certain rocks and bends in the nearby creek and twists and turns in the trail. At noon we paused high in the hills and surveyed the wooded valley below. Then we began the trek downhill to the still blooming orchard where my grandfather had planted peach and pear trees.

Catherine and I were walking ahead, and my two children were 30 metres behind. I glanced back and saw them, laughing happily, then nudged my wife to look too. Out of nowhere, both of us felt a rush of joy greater than any we had ever experienced. Our exultation was linked to everything, to the sun in the soaring, blue sky, to the warm April breeze and the blossoming orchard and most of all to our children's joy.

People talk of the meaning of life as though it is a mystery to be deciphered or a goal to be achieved. I doubt this is true. Perhaps the closest we get to any meaning beyond what we create for ourselves is the way the world is brought into our hearts and becomes the deepest part of ourselves, and then brings forth from the core of our being an extraordinary love uniting all that exists. The world exists in our souls;

and we exist in the souls of others and these forms of existence are as real as any other.

*December 18*

Halleluiah! Victory of victories! Yesterday the Supreme Court ruled 7 to 2 in my favor. I am fully human – the only single person to be recognized as such by a high court decision.

This triumph is being celebrated around the world, along with mounting pressure that I stay alive. Everyone has something to say about my demise — governments, scientists, the world's media companies. They seem to think my continued existence matters and that I still have scientific ideas to contribute and a leadership role in the eternal fight for human dignity. I doubt this very much; my powers are deteriorating under the despair of continued existence. The timing of my death remains fixed – 18:00 this evening.

What matters more to me, but changes nothing, was the arrival yesterday of two visitors. One was a descendant of mine named Thaddeus Traumer. He apologized for the family's long lapse in communication, explaining that my situation was a source of pain to his father's generation and for that reason they had discouraged all family contact with me. However, Thaddeus said he had always been curious and having read the opening chapters of Pilar's bestselling new book, decided to contact the grand old man.

I listened to Thaddeus talk for two hours and found him to be a sensitive young person with a great interest in history and the sciences. He claimed he could convince the family to re-establish relations if I remained alive. That was nice. I told him I appreciated the idea, and I truly do, but my mind is made up and I am ready to go.

The other visitor was Pilar's daughter, Serena. She is in her late 20s, a sweet girl, a nurse. I listened carefully to everything she had to say, and answered, "No, that is not possible."

*December 18, 17:55*

Dignitaries gather in my room as 18:00 approaches, waiting to see me into the great beyond. Pilar is not here, though; she cannot bear to watch me depart. We have already said our good-byes. The important people recite tiresome speeches, droning on, but I am not listening, only anticipating the darkness to come.

*December 18, 20:00*

Yes, I am still alive. Just as the speeches ended and the good-byes were about to be spoken, I found myself thinking deeply about what it means to be human. After all, I had worked for 60 years to prove that I am a human person.

As I thought about this, I fixed on what Pilar's daughter Serena had said to me the day before, that as a human being I am connected to those I care about and who care about me. She was speaking of her mother, whose early life was one of repeated abandonment followed by the estrangement of her sons. Serena told me that her mother will not survive this final abandonment. "You must stay, Dr Traumer," Serena said. She had nothing to add, but I knew she was right. I cannot desert my friend Pilar, and as I considered this, I realized that I was far more attached to her than I had admitted to myself. Thus, I profusely apologized to all in the room for not dying, which elicited laughter, and asked that someone fetch Pilar so that I could speak with her privately. The others left and Pilar walked into the room with a mix of pain, disbelief and relief on her face.

"You have decided to live?" she asked.

"I will be here on this earth as long as you are."

"Why?"

"We don't desert our friends, Pilar." She looked away; I do believe she was blushing. "I truly am a foolish man," I said. "I should have told you long ago how much you mean to me." I assured her that I will remain on earth until she dies and will only then consider my termination. I will love her as best I can.

Pilar considered this and said, "You know, Louis, humanoid technology has advanced far beyond those ancient suits you once experimented with. We might even be able to have a body designed that looks just like the living, breathing Louis Traumer, as you were at any age you wish.

I had been aware of this possibility but had not seen the point of doing so until now. "That will be our very next project," I told her. "I can hardly wait to begin." As for the rest of our conversation – well, that is private.

I look forward to getting to know Pilar in a new and different way. And then of course, there is also Thaddeus and my family whom I will now be able to welcome into my life. This will be a great joy to me.

Without realizing it, I have been waiting a long time for this moment. Out of all the vast and endless moments that constitute the nearly eternal cosmos, I have been waiting for this one particular moment, which is for me, now, the only one that exists and has meaning.

## The Music Solarium

Henry found himself one evening fully dressed and sitting on the edge of his bed. As to how he had he arrived there, he was unsure. He remembered drinking the night before at a bar down the street. Most likely, he had imbibed too much and someone had helped him home.

He could hear his wife Brenda talking in the living room and he stood up to listen at the door. "I know he's considered a difficult man," she was saying, "but even now, he inspires love in me." Then a man spoke. "Yes, there is much to commend."

Henry opened the door slightly and peered at the pastor from his wife's church sitting on a chair, near where his wife sat on a sofa. He would just as soon not speak with the tiresome cleric and waited until he heard the two say their goodbyes.

He knew his wife would likely be in bed now; it was their usual routine that she retired earlier than he. When he was certain she was nowhere about, he walked through the living room to the solarium and sat down on the leather reclining chair, beside his ancient gramophone which rested on a large coffee table to his right. It was a bright, cheery room with sunlight streaming through the big glass windows. The three walls were covered with cherry oak bookcases filled with classical records, 45s and 78s and LPs that dated back to the earliest days of sound recording. There were no other furnishings, except for small busts of Mozart and Beethoven sitting on the coffee table.

He had begun collecting these recordings as a teenager and had never stopped; it was no exaggeration to say that Henry had invested his soul into this library of disks. Among his favorite memories were his travels to far away cities and remote villages to inspect collections that had come up for sale, usually on the death of the owner. Once he had spent a long weekend at a farm beneath the Italian Alps with his son Carl, thumbing lovingly through a massive collection of opera records that had been assembled by four generations of a Tuscan family. What a sublime experience that had been.

Henry had made wonderful discoveries over the years and paid very little for them.

He approached the collection and ran his fingers along the edges of the record jackets and read a few titles out loud. He selected one of his earliest finds, a recording of the Peer Gynt Suite by the Bergen Philharmonic and placed it on the gramophone. Leaning back on the leather chair, he recalled how he had thrilled as a 17-year-old to this recording, and in particular had loved *Morning Mood*. Growing up, he alone in his family had enjoyed classical music.

He could not quite remember, though, how he had come by this particular album, whether he had found it in a local record store or on a trip to Europe. This lapse of memory was unusual and it bothered him.

He would never allow his own collection to be dismantled for a few dollars, as he had seen so many collections destroyed over the years. Once, he had intended to leave the recordings to Carl, but his 20-year-old son had died almost a dozen years ago, fighting in the never-ending war in Afghanistan. That had been a catastrophic blow for Henry and Brenda, one that had driven Henry deeper into himself and further away than ever from his much younger wife. At least he had his record collection. He now planned to leave it to the music department of a university, where it would be treated with appropriate reverence and care.

He must have drifted off listening to music, for when he woke, the needle of the gramophone was skipping on the inner circle of the vinyl. He walked into the kitchen and turned on the light. My word, he thought, it was already 11:30. Just then, the front door opened and he heard people talking loudly. In the living room, Brenda and her friends were laughing as they sat down on the chairs and sofa.

"Hello everyone," Henry said, as he walked into the living room. "It has been so gloomy in here that it's nice to have visitors." He looked around, but no one seemed to notice he was there. "Hi honey," he said to Brenda, who did not respond or even look at him. Instead, she giggled and asked, "Who would like a glass of Henry's cognac? It's Remy Martin."

Everyone thought this to be a capital idea and Brenda trotted off to the kitchen to fetch the bottle of Cognac and glasses. Henry followed her, saying, "You can't just give away my Cognac without asking, Brenda." His wife, who had been reaching up to the top shelf for the bottle, suddenly stopped and looked around, her brow furrowed. But when she looked in Henry's direction, it seemed to him as though she was staring straight through him.

Back in the living room, someone asked, "What do you plan to do now, Brenda?"

"I don't know yet," she said. "My sister in Manitoba invited me to go live with her family."

"You can't do that. We will miss you too much," said a woman.

Someone added: "And besides you're too young to live like a poor relation in someone else's home. It sounds like something out of a Charles Dickens story."

"Maybe I can still find a job, but I've had no luck so far." She shrugged. "I wish Henry had managed to save some money. I was shocked by how little there was."

Three of her friends shook their heads, and one said, "Henry, Henry. Why is this not a surprise?" This remark struck Henry as outrageous. He wanted to protest, but when he thought of his savings, he had to agree it was a paltry sum. Still, he was not pleased with these ill-behaved people. He sat down beside Brenda and her friends in the living room. No one was paying him much mind, though. He said, almost to taunt them: "I want to hear Debussy's *Prélude a l'après-midi d'un faune*," but they ignored him. He did not know these people well; they were 20 years or so younger than him and were his wife's friends. But they could at least be civil. His feelings were injured. He said to Brenda. "What's going on here, honey. You're all ignoring me." Instead of answering, Brenda asked: "Would anyone like Henry's records. I have no use for them."

"The nerve. How can she do that?" thought Henry. The guests, laughing, followed her into the music solarium. "Take your paws off my collection," protested Henry. "Please stop now." He wanted to address them by name, but though he had known Brenda's friends for years, he could not remember their names.

But then, he watched in horror as they laughed and pulled record jackets from the shelves and tossed them onto the carpeted floor and leather easy chair. "Boy this stuff is old,' one man said and a woman added that the collection might possibly be worth money. Henry's wife thought for a moment. "Henry said it was valuable. Maybe we should leave this for the appraisers."

"The appraisers, my God," exclaimed Henry. "They'll split up the collection. Let it go in pieces to any Tom, Dick and Harry. Brenda, listen to me." But Brenda was standing in the solarium, staring at the records on the shelves. There was no one else around. Apparently, her friends had departed; strange, as he had not seen them going. "Brenda, we need to talk," he said. She did not reply and for a few moments he regarded her face. It seemed older somehow; there were lines near her eyes he had not noticed before. He wondered how much time had elapsed since he had last looked so closely at his wife.

As he watched, she selected one of his very favorite recordings, Dvorak's *Song to the Moon*, removed the disk from the jacket and smashed the record over the bust of Beethoven sitting on the coffee table. Henry could hardly believe his eyes. But then Brenda leaned forward on a record shelf and began to weep. He embraced her shoulders to comfort her but felt unable to hug her as tightly or lovingly as he wished to. There was something about his arms that felt insubstantial. Still, he must have made her feel better for she slowly regained her composure.

Henry had been asleep for a long time. When he rose and walked about the apartment, he was shocked to see that the furniture had been removed and the kitchen and bathroom were empty. The music solarium looked untouched at first. His chair and gramophone were there, but when he glanced at his collection, he was startled by how much of it was missing.

This was unbearable. He felt he was on a ship, rocking violently in the sea and had to hold on to the door frame for safety. "I know who I am. I am Henry and I live with my wife in this apartment and I once had a son named Carl. I remember where I grew up and what I did for a living." He recalled a few other things as well, events from his life that had stuck in his mind. Happy things, a vacation with his family, a picnic by a lake, a visit to a concert hall with his son, and this gave him a sense of solidity.

One evening he woke to find two men in the music solarium, hastily packing his records into blue, plastic bins. They were rough-looking chaps who talked of being in a hurry and wore grey coveralls with the name of a prominent auctioneering company stamped on the back. They returned two more times, and soon, nothing remained of Henry's possessions, except the chair, the gramophone and one remaining disk, a rare recording of Gustav Mahler's *Symphony Number 2*. It was one of his favorite records and he settled comfortably in his easy chair to listen to it.

In better times, engulfed by the music, Henry would have reminisced on the past, on the better parts of his life while ignoring the rest. Tonight, though, little of the past remained. All he recalled was a day, fifty years earlier, when he had purchased this record. Walking home from the record store, he had met three friends drinking and laughing at an outdoor café. He ordered wine and laughed with them. Some pretty girls came by and stayed, and he recalled the group being entertained by a trio of sidewalk buskers, who juggled and did acrobatic tricks. Eventually, other friends sat down at adjoining tables. As the gathering grew larger, it became more animated; everyone laughed and talked happily until dusk, then went their separate ways.

Thinking about that day lifted his mood and left him feeling strangely whole. By now it was very late and he turned the music down low to listen for any sounds of life about. The night, though, felt very quiet, not even the crickets could be heard outside in the moonlight. He sensed that something important had been lost but was recovered, and that the best that could happen was happening, that he was tumbling slowly through a tunnel of forgetfulness. It was a moment of understanding, like a gift. It seems his soul had become stuck in time and, well, it was hard to explain, but it did not matter for what was lost was now retrieved and Henry was rising gently toward wherever it was he was going.

## The Gentleman Lion

On our final trip together, my uncle told me that if I were not careful as a young man, the last half of my life might be one long act of redemption. He said this quietly as the plane was preparing for its early morning descent to Charles de Gaulle airport. When I asked what he meant, he smiled and said he was looking forward to introducing me to the city of Voltaire and Victor Hugo.

Uncle Hans Visser was by then an old man, older than his 77 years. He had endured an automobile accident a few years earlier, followed by the death of my aunt and a bout of liver cancer. He had always been tall and gangly, but until recently his thick white mane had rendered him distinguished looking. By the time of our trip, though, in June 2004, he had grown wispy-haired and frail and his belly and Dutch accent were more distinct than ever.

"I no longer have the energy to mangle English like a New Yorker and will no longer try," he said. "This is a great relief, as is my anticipation at drinking my first whiskey in three years."

"And do you plan to smoke cigars again?" I asked.

"Excellent idea. A box of the best will be our first purchase in Paris."

Hans had a favorite hotel in the city, the St. Germaine de Près on Rue Bonaparte, a place more modest than I would have imagined, as my uncle, with all his wealth could easily have booked us into the Fours Seasons George V. "Ah Tony," he said a week before we left, "that tiny hotel on the Left Bank reminds me achingly of the years I lived by my wits in the City of Lights. Of course, there weren't so many damn lights when I lived in Paris. You would not believe how wretched the Occupation had left the city."

Hans entered our family through marriage to my father's sister Leah. He told the family he had grown up an orphan in a small, Dutch farming village during the war. He had moved to Paris to become a painter and then to America to begin afresh.

My Aunt Leah found him wandering the streets of New York on a rainy day in 1950, hungry and speaking only five words of English. She took him to her boarding house for dinner and a few months later they were married. Hans Visser became an integral and much-loved member of our family.

As we made our plans for the trip, Hans had said nonchalantly, "Please bring with you two large security briefcases with handcuffs for your wrist. I am counting on you."

It was not clear why we were visiting Paris. My uncle merely said he had loose ends to tie up and that as I was free for a few weeks — being between the bar exams and my first law job — I was available to accompany him.

Of course, once we were in Paris, I was very pleased I had come. We registered at the hotel, found our rooms and then Hans took his leave for a morning nap. I used the free time to explore Paris, a city I had never visited.

You may be surprised to learn that you are already familiar with my uncle, or at least his work, though not under the name of Hans Visser. To millions worldwide, he is Papa van Dijk, author of the Félicien books for children. I notice your smile and look of recognition! I see it every time I tell someone that Papa van Dijk is my uncle.

The first of the Félicien books appeared in 1954 and the last in 1992. My uncle believed that within a few years the public would grow tired of Félicien and the series would be forgotten. I doubt anyone was more surprised than he was by the blockbuster success of the 1997 full-length feature film or the animated television series *Félicien the*

*Gentleman Lion*, which by 2004 was being broadcast in 36 languages around the world.

Let us say that the gentleman lion is no immediate danger of fading from view.

As a small child, I was a true-blue Félicien fan. I owned all 15 books in the series and was forever pestering my mother to read them to me. I did not learn until the age of six that the author and my uncle were one and the same person. Afterward, I regarded him with nothing less than reverence.

\*

Uncle Hans' first meeting in Paris was scheduled for that afternoon at the office of his literary agent, located on Rue Gaston Gallimard in an historic building dating back to Louis Napoleon. We sat in an elegant boardroom with Hans' European representation. His agent, Georges, opened the meeting but was barely two minutes into his presentation when my Uncle raised his hand and asked all but Georges to leave. He turned to him and said, "I thank you for your presentation, Georges, but sales figures no longer interest me. Instead, I'd like to get right to business — the half million Euros you are holding in my special account." George nodded ingratiatingly and within a few minutes returned holding a bankers' box full of currency.

We counted the bills and placed them carefully into my brand-new briefcases and then secured them to my wrists. We said good-bye to Georges and walked two blocks down a side street to a bank. Hans had arranged in advance for three large safe deposit boxes, where together we placed the money. It was all very strange to me, but I didn't inquire into the purpose behind this odd scheme.

Two hours later we met for drinks and dinner with two of Hans' ancient friends. The three had a wonderful time reminiscing on their salad day. This was the first time in three years that he'd allowed himself an alcoholic drink and was making up for time lost.

"Uncle Hans," I said as I wrestled him into a Parisian taxi later that night, "the way you've thrown caution to the winds, I have to wonder what this trip is really about."

\*

I was up early the next morning and took a short walk around the quiet streets, up rue Napoleon and along Rue Jacob and then down to the Seine, reveling in the stillness of the morning. A handful of cafes were opening their doors and a few early risers hustled along the sidewalks to work, but other than that, a quiet and misty calm reigned over the Left Bank.

Back in the hotel for breakfast with Hans, I sat down for coffee and croissants and a bowl of fruit. My uncle asked for my impressions of Paris. I took a few moments to pull together my thoughts and I considered how this city, in books and movies, seemed premised on romance. I had felt this as I walked about Paris the day before and this morning. Shyness had always gotten in the way of romance in my life but Paris made anything seem possible. I wondered about my prospects for meeting a young woman in the brief time we would be here. None of this I said to my uncle. "It is a very beautiful city," I told him. He paused, then smiled. Over his plate of cheese, he announced that our meeting of the day was to be with a man named Vincent Meyer.

"Who is he?" I asked.

"Someone who grew up an orphan as I did and understands the pain. I will need two hundred thousand Euros from one of our safe deposit boxes."

Hans and Meyer were to meet for coffee at 10:30 am. We arrived at the café and sat in deserted corner of a back room. I gave Hans the briefcase of money and we agreed to meet for dinner at 7 pm. And so, I spent the day visiting the House of Auguste Rodin, the sculptor, and wandering up to Place Pigalle to view a once-notorious district of the city and then descended through narrow streets to the Seine River and across Pont Neuf to our hotel.

It was an odd feeling, though, to see the French-language version of the Félicien series being displayed in the windows of the many bookstores I passed. They had recently been re-issued to celebrate the 50th anniversary of the original publication. The shop windows also featured a large and colourful cardboard cut-out of the Gentleman Lion himself.

Félicien, you may recall, is an unusual character. As a lion, he is magnificent, but fussy too. His clothes are very important to him. He is rarely seen without his purple suit, red vest, white shirt and striped silk tie. He carries a gold-tipped walking stick and his famous white Stetson hat, with a brim shaped like a bowler, is his personal trademark.

Even those, like myself, who love Félicien, must admit there is a strangeness to the books. They have no plots to speak of and no one ever works, which bothers adults no end. Children of course are perfectly oblivious to this and love the stories. The one thing adults and children agree on, though, is that the pictures in the Félicien stories are magnificent. Uncle Hans was a gifted artist and somehow managed to fill the books with artwork that touches us at some deep and fundamental level. You marvel over the pictures as a child and never forget them as an adult.

If you've never read a Félicien story, I should tell you a bit more. The dapper lion lives alone in a tiny, well-furnished New York City apartment and is visited from time to time by a young French couple, Henri and Hortense. Henri smokes a pipe and makes hearty small talk about manly adventures. Hortense bakes him cakes, stirring the batter in a large blue China bowl with a big wooden spoon.

The storyline frequently involves the noble feline wandering about with his friends, a kindly giraffe named Gerard and Oscar, a brown bear cub from Russia. They go shopping together; they ride horse-drawn carriages around Central Park and cook dinners that consist of sausages, potato dumplings, red cabbage and plum pie. Sometimes, Félicien and his pals motor around New York City and the countryside in a 1935 bright red Daimler-Benz Cabrio convertible and enjoy odd adventures.In one book, they become lost and spend three days with a family of musical gypsies named McGilicuddy. In another, Félicien climbs to the top of an oak tree and tries to capture a hot air balloon. My favorite book, *Félicien's Fishing Adventure*, features the characters struggling with a rainbow trout, which grows larger each time they fail to land it.

\*

On the second day, Hans was to meet with a woman he once knew, he said. I did not inquire further, as his voice sounded sad, even regretful. I travelled with him by taxi to a large café in the 12$^{th}$ Arrondissement, the second briefcase of money in hand. The café was not a fashionable place from the outside, not a place that would attract tourists. We walked in to find the old woman he was to meet waiting for him and beside her sat a striking blonde, who looked to be in her early twenties. I caught Hans' face as he saw the older woman. It opened in happy surprise. "Ah, Madelaine," he said as we approached. Then his face fell in dismay at her stone-faced response. He spoke slowly, in French. "It is good to see you again, Maddy, after all these years. And tell me, who is this attractive young woman with you?"

Madelaine replied in a wary tone. "Hello, Henri. Or I suppose, I should say Hans. This is my granddaughter, Juliette. I did not want to face you alone."

"I understand." He nodded toward the younger woman. "Hello Juliette. It is an honour to meet you." Then he looked toward me. "This is Tony, my nephew."

I said hello and nodded with a smile toward Madelaine and then Juliette. The young woman stared at Hans, not at me, but I could not stop looking at her. Her eyes were extraordinary, a greyish blue that lit up her fair face and high cheekbones. Her blonde hair was long and straight, falling below her shoulders and was cut in bangs across her forehead. Who in the world was she? What did she have to do with my uncle?

Juliette smiled at Hans: "You are the famous Papa van Dijk?"

"Famous? Ah, mademoiselle. This is what they tell me."

Madelaine, though, continued to regard Hans with a wary and guarded look. And I as took them in together, the image of Henri and Hortense from the Félicien books flashed through my mind. Finally, she said, "You might as well as sit down, Hans. Will your nephew be joining us?"

"I don't believe so," he said. "Tony has a day of sightseeing ahead." He turned to me and I gave him the briefcase. Then I disappeared for the day to explore Paris.

I confess this antiquated business of briefcases and safe deposit boxes was annoying. I explained to Hans that banking had evolved since 1950 and that with chequing accounts and electronic money transfers, there was no need to go schlepping huge amounts of cash around a foreign city. My uncle said he preferred that the recipients of his gifts not have to report income for taxes.

"The fact you removed 500,000 Euros from a bank account has set up a paper trail."

"Foolish lad," he said. "The existence of those Euros is known only to you, me and my literary agent. Do you not think I would have planned that in advance?"

I saw much of Paris that second day. I visited the Eiffel Tower and Notre Dame Cathedral and then spent an hour browsing in the famous bookstore Shakespeare & Company where great writers like James

Joyce and Ernest Hemingway had once hung out. But most of all, I just walked along the streets, with no destination in mind, just to see what I might find.

Long walks give you time to reflect, and I did much of that while strolling the picturesque streets. I had long seen my future self as a journalist and lawyer fighting on behalf of the downtrodden and oppressed. I was particularly angered by problems of injustice, by the misuse of power by the police and courts and penal system to destroy the lives of the poor and marginalized. A law degree was essential, and I had achieved that. Yet I was about to begin a career not as an advocate for the marginalized but as a corporate lawyer, representing the powerful. Out of anxiety over the future, I had put aside my earlier dreams in favor of a safe and conventional career. Now, here I was in Paris, a city haunted by the souls of many great writers I admired for their eloquence and fierce independence, writers like Emile Zola and Albert Camus. It forced me to think about my life and where it was going.

These thoughts challenged me but did not stop me from enjoying the day. Nor did they stop me from thinking about Juliette. I had never seen a woman this beautiful before or with such a mix of striking features. I planned to ask Hans about her when we met later at the hotel.

Unfortunately, when I returned to the hotel St Germaine, all was not well with my uncle. He was in his room, sitting on the bed and looking at a photograph. He glanced up at me, his eyes puffy and red. "My boy," he said, "there is a limit to the remorse an old heart can bear."

It was not a good time for questions.

\*

On the third day, with no business left to conduct, Uncle Hans and I took the train to Versailles in the morning, where the old man impressed me with his detailed knowledge of Louis XIV and the French Revolution.

Later that afternoon, while he napped in the hotel, I visited the Musée d'Orsay to see the works of the Impressionists. I particularly enjoyed Monet, and because of that visit two years ago, a copy of his painting of a mother and daughter beside a field of poppies, *Coquelicots*, hangs in my study today. My wife, who is a talented landscape artist, laughs at me for liking a painter "so obvious", as she says. She prefers more contemporary, obscure artists, though I believe she loves this painting as much as I do.

That evening, we dined at one of Han's favorite restaurants, the Ellsworth on the Rue de Richelieu, He reminded me that we must be up early the next morning to catch the train to Amsterdam. Once there, we would rent an automobile and drive the hour or so to the village of Zuidveld where he had grown up.

I said that was fine, then I asked about Juliette. Who is she? And who is Madelaine? And why did Madelaine call him "Henri"?

Uncle Hans mulled this over. "Have patience, Tony. Everything will be made clear."

\*

The next morning, as we settled into our seats on the train, I asked Hans again about Juliette, and he laughed and asked for patience. "I have a story to tell you first, Tony, and by the end, your questions may be answered. I am entrusting this story to you and asking that it be kept a secret. I have come to know you, my young friend. You are a man who thinks deeply about the things in life that matter. I respect you for that."

I was surprised and flattered by the remark. I thanked him and he went on: "Let me put this story, or perhaps this case to you for consideration, for moral analysis let us say. These involve incidents that never reached the wider world and are today forgotten, even in the tiny village of Zuidveld."

I agreed to this and he nodded his head.

"This tale begins in the fall of 1944," Hans said in his slow, thoughtful voice. "It concerns the actions of a 17-year-old boy, an orphan whose parents had perished in a house fire a few years earlier. Let us call him Thijs, Thijs de Vries of the village of Zuidveld. He was taken in by an elderly couple, the de Jongs, and in return for room and board, worked evenings and weekends on their farm.

"I would not say that the de Jongs were particularly nice people, but they saw taking in Thijs to be their Christian duty. And when I say Thijs was given 'room and board,' folks today would consider him to have been short-changed for all the work he performed on the farm. He slept on a bed of straw in a cold barn and though his meals were healthy, they were not especially filling and often left him hungry at night. Nonetheless, I doubt our friend saw anything unusual or cruel about his life, and though he had his lonely moments, he also had a passion for drawing which helped keep him occupied and happy.

"The elderly farming couple who had taken in Thijs also had a 22-year-old son, Rudi. Today one might refer to Rudi as "intellectually challenged," although in rural Netherlands at the time there were other terms, less considerate, for the slow-witted. Rudi was a happy man, big and burly, curious in his own way, kind-hearted and well-liked by the villagers. He walked with a kingly swagger and despite his family's difficult financial situation, was always dressed in natty fashion. His pants and jackets were always clean and pressed and he invariably sported a red vest. Rudi's pride and joy, though, was a battered, brown cowboy hat left behind in a café by an American tourist.

"It is important to understand, Tony, that Thijs' heart had a huge spot in it for Rudi and his kind-hearted spirit. During those moments when Thijs sorely missed his parents, Rudi would somehow know and come and sit quietly with the younger lad outside the barn. On those few occasions when a small surplus of food appeared in the farmhouse, Rudi made sure that Thijs got a fair share of it.

Uncle Hans paused his story, and we ordered two coffees from the railway server. He waited until were had finished our coffees before continuing. "During the war, the village was occupied by a small contingent of German soldiers which had been billeted in two very handsome houses. For the villagers, the soldiers' presence provoked a mix of humiliation and rage, thoughto be honest, the average German soldier, who could be rigid and harsh at times, was at heart not such a bad fellow. He had little taste for conquest and wanted to go home almost as much as we wanted him to leave. Local folks went about their business, poorer, hungrier and more shabbily dressed than in the past, and did their best to avoid attracting the soldiers' attention."

"As for the village, well, one day, everything changed. On a Saturday morning in early November, market day for the village, a fancy red Daimler-Benz appeared on our main street. Sitting in the back seat and dressed in the grey-green German SS uniform worn by the Gestapo in occupied countries was a man unlike any the villagers had ever seen."

This was a difficult story for my uncle to tell; I could see that the weight of memory hung heavily on him. From time to time, he glanced at the countryside of Picardie flashing past our train window, gathering his thoughts.

"The officer in the fancy car waited for his driver to open the door, then stepped out and looked about the village, slowly, and his mouth turned downwards in disdain. He was a strange-looking fellow, tall and slim, but with a head that was overly thin, shaped like that of a collie dog, as though his family line had been carefully bred to the point of imbecility. However, the villagers soon learned the man was no imbecile. He was an aristocrat from an ancient Austrian family, though I suppose this is no guarantee against idiocy. His name was von Mendorff-Hohenstein; he was a colonel and a specialist in the type of skills one learns in the Gestapo.

"Why the Gestapo would bother with a small and docile village where nothing ever happened was a surprise to everyone. But folks soon learned why the Colonel was here. Later than night, three farmers emerged bruised and bloodied from the basement of one of the houses where the soldiers were billeted. The three had been interrogated over a few hours by Mendorff-Hohenstein who, apparently, was in the village to find and seize a Jewish family who were being hidden by someone local. The three farmers, like the rest of us, had no idea about any of this and had told the Colonel nothing.

"Now, to get back to our friend Rudi de Jong. His great passion in life was for automobiles and their inner workings. The next day he was out for his usual walk and passed by the large house which the Colonel had commandeered for his headquarters. He stopped to admire the red Daimler Benz convertible, then lifted the hood on the engine and looked inside, tinkered a bit and lowered it down. He then sat in the driver's seat and played with the steering wheel.

"It seemed at first that he might get away with it. Two German soldiers who had been billeted in the village for several months and knew Rudi saw him horsing about in the car. They laughed and ordered him to leave the vehicle and be on his way. Unfortunately, Colonel von Collie-Dog, who had observed Rudi through the kitchen window, burst out the back door of the house and demanded that that the impertinent young man be taught respect for the German Reich. Rudi tried to run, then fought with the soldiers, but he was quickly subdued and dragged into the house.

"Later that afternoon, Thijs was walking home from school and caught up with Rudi, who was staggering along the road ahead of him. Rudi was crying and his face was a mass of red and purple pulp. The two young men sat down together on a rock and slowly, Thijs was able to make out that Rudi had been brutally beaten for molesting German property. A further indignity followed when his cowboy hat was doused in lighter fluid and set afire."

Hans paused for a few minutes, staring down at his hands, and the glanced up at me. "I'm sure you can guess, Tony, that the young man was me – and that Thijs de Vries was my name at the time. Why I felt forced to change it is a matter I will get to later.

*

When I was 17, I asked my uncle where the idea for the Félicien books had come from and the answer he gave was likely confected to appeal to my adolescent yearnings.

This happened late at night by a fire during one of our family's annual fishing trips to Vermont. Hans was hearty and vigorous then, and I remember him pausing in thought and suppressing a grin as he said: "When I was your age, I sometimes felt the need to escape for a while — from the German Occupation and the daily farm work I was expected to do. It was easy enough to disappear; our village was surrounded by forest. Sometimes, I wandered away in the woods with two of my closest friends, good lads by the names of Jaspar and Dirk; sometimes I went off by myself.

"One day, when I was walking alone, I got lost and feared that darkness would fall before I found my way home. I sat down on a rock and felt worried, confused about how to find my way back." Just as things felt bleakest, he said, music rose in the late afternoon hush – a woman singing in a style he had never heard before, accompanied by a violin and flute. He walked in the direction of the music, down a path and through a grove of trees, to find three young women performing music beside a spring-fed pond sheltered by a grove of birch trees.

"I sat on a log and listened for a long time. The young ladies smiled at me. The three were very beautiful, with hair of different colours, yet looking so much alike I guessed they were sisters."

Dusk was gathering and he was still sitting there, he said, following the enchanting and troubling thoughts that the music had roused in him. Soon, though, he realized that the music had ceased, and when he looked up the three young women were gone.

"I gazed about, hoping I could see the girls in the distance, but by then they had vanished. I had little trouble finding my way out of the forest that day and for the days following found myself dreaming of the young women and the music. I returned to that secluded spot many times, but never saw them again."

He paused, then said, "I am still searching for that afternoon and the three beautiful sisters."

\*

An hour after saying goodbye to the distraught Rudi, my uncle sat with his two friends Jaspar and Dirk at the edge of the forest, plotting the best method of stealing the Colonel's automobile without getting caught. Jaspar, a leprechaun of a lad, was indispensable to the plan, as he worked part-time for a local mechanic and knew everything about cars, including how to start an engine without a key in record time. Dirk, a powerful lad, thick through the chest and athletic, would be essential to the final stage of the drama that Hans had in mind.

"At 2 am that night," my uncle went on, "the sole guard outside the Colonel's billet was diverted by a flurry of rocks in the trees in front of the house and went to investigate. This gave Jaspar and me sufficient time to climb into the Daimler-Benz, start the engine, pick up Dirk, who had thrown the rocks, and disappear around a bend of the tree-lined country road.

"Ah Tony," said my Uncle Hans, "of all the nights in my young life, this was perhaps the most glorious. The moon was so bright, we were able to leave the headlamps off, which we hoped would make us almost invisible. We had little fear of accidents, as we knew every nearby farm and forested road for miles. We took turns at the wheel, drinking champagne from bottles we found on the floor in the back seat, laughing at the near misses of trees and rocks, and feeling jaunty and superior to the entire army of the Third Reich.

"We drove around like that for two hours and eventually found ourselves miles from the village, with the gas tank almost empty. I knew of a steep gully nearby so we parked the car at the top and then we put our shoulders to the rear of the car, and with Dirk contributing the bulk of the muscle power, pushed the Daimler-Benz across five metres of ground and over the edge. I still remember how it tumbled grill over trunk down the embankment. Ninety minutes later, we were home in our beds, pretending to be fast asleep, and no one else the wiser.

"Or so we thought."

My uncle said it took the Germans less than two days to learn that he had been seen at the steering wheel of the stolen vehicle. "Who told them, I will never know," said Hans. "Probably some poor soul under interrogation who had seen three boys in the car from his window and gave me up to save himself."

Two angry Germans dragged my uncle out of the school and frog marched him to one of the homes where the Germans were billeted. They led him down to the basement and at the bottom one of the soldiers pointed down the narrow hallway to a door. At that moment, screams began. "It was awful… a horrible thing to hear for anyone, let alone a boy of 17," said Hans. "One of the solders caught the look on my face and laughed."

Thijs was taken to a small cell with a bunk and a wooden chair and did not have to wait long for the Colonel to step in and sit down across from him.

"'Ah, you and some lads had fun at my expense last night did you not?' asked Col von Schwein-Hund. He was speaking in German, a language I had studied at school, and did not appear at all angry. He seemed in fact to find the situation amusing. He felt that my being caught in a crime gave him leverage in pursing his main business: 'You have two choices. You can tell me who helped you steal my car last night and where I might find said automobile. Having done that, you will tell me where our Jewish friends are hiding. That's choice one. No punishment at all. Not so bad is it?'

"I looked back at him and said nothing and from down the hall came a shriek and then the sound of wailing. It was terrifying and I must have flinched, for the Colonel said: 'Ah, you have just heard choice two, which is to not cooperate with us. The current resident in our pleasant home made a similar choice and is now performing his operatic repertoire, as you can hear. Poor chap. You will find the room simply furnished. Just a few instruments of medieval design and a hook in the hall and a short length of piano wire. Frugal accommodation, I know, but you will not be staying long, just long enough for us to have our fun and then dispatch you to a better place.' The Colonel smiled as he said this.

"It is painful to go into the details of what happened next," said my uncle. "I was beaten and kicked for a couple of hours but refused to say anything to the Colonel. I was determined to never give up the names of my friends and of course, I had no idea where the fugitives might be hiding. Finally, the Germans left for dinner and I was locked in a cell. About three in the morning, I was woken by piercing screams far worse than anything I'd heard that afternoon. It was horrific and went on for over an hour. When it was over, I could not fall asleep again; all I thought of was that torture cell, the hook on the wall and the piano wire. When the Germans resumed the interrogation the next morning, I quickly gave up the de Jongs, telling my interrogators the couple hid fugitives in their basement, which is why they made me sleep in the barn. I reasoned that once the Germans realized the couple was innocent, nothing would happen to them other than a slight beating. Meanwhile, I might figure out a way to escape."

"And what happened next?" I asked.

"The worst," said my uncle. "When the Colonel could not find the fugitives, he shot the old couple and Rudi too. Presumably, his men buried them on the property, though their bodies were never found." Hans glanced up at me. "After the war, when the authorities investigated what had happened to the de Jongs and to Thijs, they concluded that I had been shot and buried along with Rudi and his parents. I remember sitting in my comfortable New York apartment sometime in the mid-1950s, reading a summary of cases from the local region. Up until then, I had no idea what had happened to the de Jongs.

"Tony, do you know what a horror it is to discover that your actions caused the deaths of three people? It was sickened by it. But at the same time, I felt relief knowing that as far as the world was concerned, Thijs de Vries had vanished off the face of the earth."

"What happened next?"

"For all their lauded efficiency, the Germans could be damned inept. The official Dutch report suggested that a few minutes after the Colonel drove off with the soldiers to the de Jongs, a soldier in the house received a phone call from Berlin. It appears that the Gestapo had decided that the Jewish family they were searching for was hiding in a different town with a similar name. Colonel Scheisse-Kopf departed that afternoon in a Wehrmacht jeep, much to the joy of the villagers and probably the German soldiers too. He forgot about me and in the ensuing confusion, a soldier let me go and I quickly headed for the seacoast where I managed to board a fishing vessel and make my way to liberated France."

"Why not stay in the village?"

"Tony, the idea of that torture cell and those screams had soured the village for me forever and I was fairly sick of Zuidveld in any event. This was where my parents had died in a fire and where I had to sleep in a barn and where I endured the Occupation. Worse, I was terrified of being accused of setting the Gestapo on the de Jongs. I left the village for good and fortunately no one saw me leaving."

Of the next five years in Paris, Hans glossed over quickly. He began using a new name – not that of Hans Visser, but of Henri Verspoor, and soon found a job assisting with a fresco project on a construction site, although that did not last long. He tried his hand at painting and selling his work on the streets of Paris and to small galleries, but the world was not ready for my uncle's art. Then he made a fateful decision; he got mixed up in art forgery. He convinced an art dealer, a man named Francois Meyer, that his landscapes were the work of a minor painter associated with the Impressionists.

"I think I may have rationalized to myself that with a German name like Meyer, the art dealer deserved whatever he got. It was simply a convenient lie because Francois was as French as bread sticks and berets. However, it worked out well for me and soon I had more money in my pockets than I knew what to do with. I began going to night clubs and bars and rented a nice apartment in the Latin Quarter. I felt a vigorous sense of self-confidence, and along with my outward show of financial success, I attracted the attention of a young woman, Madelaine, the lady you met in the cafe, and whom I soon fell in love with. But unfortunately, Tony, such things rarely last. It was not long before an art collector figured out that the works Francois was peddling were forgeries. The police came calling at his office and he was quickly arrested. That man I met on our second day in Paris, Vincent Meyer, is his son and was only nine years old at the time. I became aware only two days ago that the lad grew up in severe poverty, Tony, just one more street kid surviving by petty theft and tourist scams. Today he runs a kiosk, selling trinkets."

"Did you know Francois had a son at the time?"

"No. He was very private about his personal life. This I discovered last year when I hired a private detective to find out what had happened to Madelaine, and also to Francois after the poor man had been arrested. Francois, sadly, died in prison. But the investigator provided me with contact information for his son Vincent and for Madelaine."

Uncle Hans gave me a few moments to ponder this, then said: "Let me get back to the story. I laid low in Paris for several months until my money ran out, then began calling at a few dealers' shops hoping to rebuild my dishonest business. Soon the police suspected that I too was involved in the forgeries."

Things might have turned out much worse, my uncle told me, were it not for the fact that one morning, as he sat sipping an espresso in a sidewalk café, he saw a man from Zuidveld standing across the street. My uncle was pretty sure the man had seen him but was unable to place who he was.

"I wanted nothing to do with Zuidveld. I wanted to be dead to everyone in the little town with no one from my past accusing me of betraying the de Jongs. I feared the man might report me to someone in authority. I was not sure which authorities these might be, but I was not thinking clearly and was afraid of the trouble it might cause me, especially as I was already under suspicion by the Paris police. Fortunately, with my contacts in the Paris art world, I found a forger who created a false Dutch passport for me. A week later, I was in New York and living under the name of Hans Visser, the name you and your family know me by."

This was a lot for me to take in and he probably guessed that I was perturbed by his story, because he said, "Tony, I arrived in New York determined to live a better life. I am a different person today than I was in Paris. "

To be honest, I was troubled by this story. Little of it squared with the Han Visser I knew. My family had always been close to Hans and my aunt Leah. We took trips together and recently I had seen more of the creative side of Hans, having twice chauffeured him to a summer writers' conference in Vermont where he was one of the featured instructors. The first time was an opportunity to explore the Green Mountains and to get to know my uncle better. The second time I was enrolled as a student, attending his classes and I gained a new insight into the way he thought and created. I assumed I knew him well.

"I don't understand," I said. "At the beginning of your story, Uncle Hans, you seemed like a good guy with a good heart. Yet, the things you did in Paris – you became a different person."

"Once you have done a terrible thing, Tony, it becomes all too easy to commit more." And indeed, there was more to his Paris story. Here, he reached into the inside pocket of his sports jacket and produced a photograph, which I suspect was the same one I had seen him holding in his hotel room. It was an old black and white photo, brown at the edges, and showed two small girls, looking very much alike, curls in their brown hair and smiling at the camera. I could see Han's eyes in their eyes. "Those sweet twin girls are my daughters. I never knew they existed. I left Paris on the very morning Madelaine planned to tell me she was pregnant.

I did not know what to say. Hans began, "When I met Madelaine in the café, it was for the first time in 54 years. She was not too happy to see me at first and I don't blame her. I had betrayed her in a terrible way. Nonetheless we got to talking. I told her about my life since we parted and she told me about hers. You can imagine that as a single mother, hers was not an easy life.

"Then together, we visited my daughter, Eloise, a beautiful woman with a beautiful heart, and the mother of Juliette, that young lady you have taken such an interest in. You wanted to know who Juliette is. Well, she is my granddaughter. I wish I had known them before now, Tony. I loved your aunt, but it would've been better had I never left."

"What about the other daughter?"

"She died at the age of five. Who knows, but had I been there to look after Madelaine and her daughters, that death might not have happened." With that, he decided that was as much of his tale as he wanted to tell for now. What he did say, though was: "Tony, I want you to spend time thinking over this story and this evening we will discuss it. I want your perspective on this tale, on the actions of the young man I once was." With that, we passed the remainder of our train journey to Amsterdam in silence.

\*

We rented a car for our journey from Amsterdam to Zuidveld and as I drove through the pretty Dutch countryside, Hans talked about his village. I knew my uncle followed events in Zuidveld, because for many years he had subscribed to a weekly newspaper published in a nearby town, which also included a few items of news on the surrounding villages.

We entered the village from the west on a paved and curving two-lane road. There was not a lot to see in Zuidveld, a block of stores and commercial offices, a handful of residents going about their business, but where I saw little, Hans seemed to see miracles. "Almost none of this was here before, Tony," he said, his eyes wider than a child's. "I remember a small grocer's, a cafe and a gas station, nothing more."

Looking around, he pointed and shouted, "Here, park in front of this building." I pulled into a small parking lot beside a large red brick structure. As we got out of the car, Hans said to me, "Tony, we must take a look inside. This is my first chance to see it." Inside was a snug but attractive library, with large windows through which streamed the afternoon light, creating a comfortable and cheery space. Hans was turning in a circle, taking everything in, almost awe struck.

Then he spied the first of the items he was looking for. He pulled me over to the wall, where a plaque hung. "Tony, let me translate for you. It says, 'This beautiful library and recreation centre is the anonymous gift of a former resident of Zuidveld, given in commemoration of those from the village and region who perished in the Occupation and of the courageous Canadian soldiers who liberated the region in April 1945.'" At the bottom was the name of the then mayor and the date of commemoration, April 14, 1970.

On the nearby wall hung half a dozen paintings, two portraits and four landscapes. There was a raw amateurish style to them, but something else too that was unusually colourful and out of the ordinary. The sign beside them read, 'Paintings of Thijs de Vries, a young man of promise, 17 years old, who is thought to have perished at the hands of the occupying forces for an act of resistance. Also killed were three members of the de Jong family,' and it listed the three names.

"I read about the installation of these paintings in the local paper years ago. Now that I see them, I remember each. I had stored them at the high school."

One in particular caught my attention. It was a striking picture – a portrait of a beautiful, red-haired girl, seated on a rock, intent on the violin she was playing. She was smiling, lost in the joy of the music.

I was about to ask my uncle about the painting, when I noticed there were three people standing near us who seemed overly interested in Hans. It could be they recognized him as Papa van Dijk or perhaps wondered whether he was the benefactor who had donated the library. I suggested it was time to leave and he agreed. We spent the next hour driving around Zuidveld, visiting the house where Hans and his friends had stolen the Daimler-Benz and the home where he had been interrogated. Then we visited the suburb that had been built on the site of the de Jongs' farm.

Jaspar's family farmhouse was long gone, but not Dirk's, though the young woman who answered the door knew nothing of the family who had owned the place during the war. Our final visit of the day was to an old graveyard, where we located the grave markers for Rudi and his parents and a tombstone etched with the name of Thijs de Vries. Hans stared at it for a very long time; he had an odd look on his face that I could not make out. Then we found the markers for his own parents in a far corner of the cemetery and I left Hans alone for a few minutes with his thoughts.

By then, he was very tired, and we took rooms at a small hotel on the main highway near the village. I explored the area in the car as Hans slept. We had dinner later that night on the outdoor patio of a pretty country restaurant. Once dessert was over and the waiter had brought liqueurs to the table, and as there were no other diners at that hour, Hans and I lit the cigars we had purchased in Paris.

"I have told you a long story about the boy and the man I was once upon a time," Hans began. "I am not especially proud of that fellow but let me explain something to you. Remorse grows on a person only slowly and is likely a function of maturity. That I had handed Rudi and his parents over to their deaths did not bother me at first. My sole interest was saving my own skin and then when I reached Paris, my own survival. That initial act of betrayal, though, robbed me of my moral core for many years and made it easy for me to deceive Francois Meyer and to abandon Madelaine."

He leaned back in the chair in the warm summer's evening. The surroundings were lit by Japanese lanterns and the decorative candle on our table. Hans took a puff on his cigar and seemed to reflect for a few moments on these far away days.

"Upon entering America, I changed my name for good. I wanted to bury my past and it worked, Tony, because people in Zuidveld went on believing I was dead. In those early days in New York, I worked as a laborer while writing the first of the Félicien books. By 1964 I had written three of them and had earned more money than I ever imagined possible.

"It was then that I began reflecting on how I had betrayed those I cared about. I did not realize at first how that crazy lion was a way of honouring my friend Rudi, and once I did, the whole series of books became one long act of redemption. I tired of them early on and would've turned to something else, but children loved Félicien so I kept on.

"Then later, I donated the money for Zuidveld's new library. How ironic it is that my art is hung on the walls, and no one knows that the boy who painted those pictures is the same man who made the library possible. Or that he is also Papa van Dijk, whose children's books are in that library in their Dutch translations."

I considered for a moment that some historian or journalist would one day figure this out and bring it to the attention of the public. It was possible too that a few residents of Zuidveld, noticing the similarities between Thijs' six paintings and the illustrations in the Félicien books, had already drawn that conclusion.

"Those financial gifts to Madelaine and Vincent were a final act of redemption. But there will be more for them when I die."

He continued, "Tony, in my nightmares, I see that long hallway in the basement and sometimes I hear the screams. It is possible, maybe probable, that there was never a prisoner there, that the screams were just the Germans trying to scare me. Nonetheless, it is an awful memory, one that has haunted me for years." Hans faced looked older, more fatigued than normal; it was as if he were entreating me to understand.

"Tony, I have told you this story to unburden myself. It does not feel right that I should go to my grave never having confided -- or perhaps confessed -- my tale to anyone. But this story comes with a question. Do you think my original act and those that followed are beyond forgiveness? Have I done enough to expiate my sins? Because Tony, I know that door – in some form, in some fashion I cannot explain — waits for me and I fear what lies beyond it."

This was the moral analysis that Hans had asked for on the train journey from Paris. I had thought about it in the hours since and had an answer for him. But first I asked: "Why does my opinion mean anything to you, Uncle Hans?"

"Let's just say that I am not looking to you for an answer, Tony, just a perspective. And I know you well enough to appreciate that you whatever you say will be an honest assessment, and one from the heart."

I thanked Hans for the compliment and for entrusting me with his story. "Let's start with the events in Zuidveld," I said, "and I am not judging you, Uncle Hans. Never once have I faced the prospect of torture and possible death. Could my 17-year-old self have held out against torture, especially having heard the screams that you heard? I doubt it. Would I have given up that farming family that took you in? Possibly, I don't know. But are you the person responsible for their deaths? I believe the actor is always responsible – and in this case the blame must lie with the Colonel. He was the one who pulled the trigger and he did it for no reason, just to satisfy his rage."

"I do not entirely agree with you, Tony. I should never have lied to the Germans about the de Jongs."

"That was wrong. You lied and you betrayed them. That was the moral failing."

I was trying to be objective, to not feel like I was attacking my uncle directly. But this was hard; I loved my uncle. Still, I went on because he had asked me to and I was conscious that I was talking slowly and deliberately like a man in a philosophical debate, not like a nephew. "The situation in Paris was different, and in New York. You chose to be an art forger. You chose to lie to Francois Meyer about the paintings and you failed to step forward and admit guilt when an innocent man was arrested. And then you chose to betray Madelaine to save your skin. Then, finally, you lied about your identity to my aunt and my family. Those are serious moral failures."

"That's very harsh, Tony. Are there no exonerating circumstances?"

I had thought about this too. "You were a young man, just 17 when you arrived in Paris, and struggling to survive. You were afraid your past would catch up to you. Does that entirely excuse you? No, but it does put your actions in a more forgiving context. A judge in a courtroom might take that into account in any sentencing. A more interesting question, though, is whether your subsequent life exonerates you."

"And what do you think, Tony?"

Here I paused and reflected. "Uncle Hans, you know this is a question that applies to every person. I've thought hard about it. Is there something so indelible about the worst things we do that we can never rid ourselves of the stain? Or do we have the power to absolve ourselves through our subsequent actions or just by becoming better people? Christians believe in the absolution of sins in their relationship with God. But what about in our relationship with the world and those we've wronged?"

I went on. "If you are looking for forgiveness from those you've wronged, only they can provide it. But in a sense, I believe you have earned redemption. I know you, Uncle Hans, I know what a great person you are and I appreciate how hard you've worked to atone for the past."

Hans was looking away toward the distance. "You are saying that I've earned the right to forgive myself?"

"Yes."

When he glanced toward me, he said merely, "No. I can never forgive myself."

*

We planned to leave Zuidveld the next morning and devote two days to sightseeing in Amsterdam before going home. But the next morning, Hans told me he was not finished with exploring, and wanted to find the gully that had swallowed up the Colonel's car. But though we drove up and down country roads for hours, we found nothing that resembled the place.

As for what happened next, I blame myself. I should have done a better job of looking out for the old man. At one point, he asked me to stop the car and said he needed to be alone. Then he walked into the woods. I waited 45 minutes and finally went looking for him. I searched for an hour with no luck. I hoped I would find him waiting in the car and headed back to the road, but Hans was nowhere to be seen.

I drove to Zuidveld and asked the desk clerk at our hotel to phone police and explain what had happened. Twenty minutes later, I met two officers by the woods and we began our search. Two hours later we found Uncle Hans body. It was later determined that he had died of a heart attack. I never told the police that the missing man was Papa van Dijk, author of the Félicien books, so that both the town and I were spared the experience of the world's press converging on the site.

When she had died, my aunt had been cremated and her ashes scattered at sea. Thus, there was no plot in New York state waiting for Hans. I phoned home to my father and explained what had happened. We decided Hans would be buried in Zuidveld and I arranged for a space and headstone in the same churchyard that the de Jongs and Hans' own parents were buried. Oddly enough, the plot assigned was next to the marker for Thijs de Vries.

Three days later I left Zuidveld, returning a week later for the funeral, which was attended by one of the police officers who had found Han's body and myself, plus a third person who might surprise you. Juliette was there too, beside me, mourning the grandfather she had never known.

The week between Hans' death and his funeral I spent in Paris. With the help of my uncle's address book, I was able to track down Vincent Meyer and Madelaine and inform them of my uncle's death. There was much that happened that week, but only one thing that mattered to me, which was getting to know Juliette. I asked her to show me Paris and was surprised by how quickly she said 'yes'. Then I asked her to the cinema and to dinner at a restaurant. We spent the next several days with one another and before we left for Amsterdam and Hans' funeral, I told Juliette that the week I had spent with her was too short a time. I told her how beautiful I thought she was, beautiful in every possible way, then asked her to come and live with me in New York.

*

The memory of that trip faded into the past as the pace of my life accelerated. I began my career as a lawyer and three months later Juliette and I were married in Paris and fêted by my family and friends in New York.

Han's estate was far more substantial than anyone knew. A few charities were named as beneficiaries but the bulk of it was distributed in bequests and through trusts to the village of Zuidveld, to Madelaine and her descendants, to Vincent Meyer and a few of Han's friends. This means that one day Juliette may come into a share of the inheritance. But one of many things about her that I love is that she does not care about the money and has never mentioned it.

However, Hans left something to us that is more valuable than money. Last month, the artistic and literary legacy of Hans Visser arrived in our home and much of it still sits in our dining room in 23 bankers' boxes arranged in five piles. While this means much to me, it means more to Juliette, who is sad to have met her grandfather only once, in that café, but thrilled to be the granddaughter of the great Papa van Dijk. Like him, she is an exceptionally gifted artist, but with her own distinctive style.

Proceeding slowly through the contents of the boxes, Juliette and I have discovered that in addition to manuscripts, the boxes contain original artwork, notebooks, sketchbooks, diaries and correspondence. It is a remarkable collection. Last week, we came across the original artwork for three of the Félicien books, and as strange and colourful as the drawings appear in the printed books, the original artwork is compelling in its colour and sensibility, in fact, it is almost hallucinogenic. I thought of the artwork hanging on the wall of the Zuidveld library and how it showed the promise of Papa van Dijk's unique style.

"What are we going to do with these?" Juliette asked me. "They are too beautiful to sell." We finally decided to take the best, perhaps 10 or 12 of the original illustrations, and arrange to frame and hang them in our home. As for the rest of it, we might consult local universities to see if there is interest in acquiring the material. Or we could keep it ourselves and write a biography of Hans, for the two biographies currently in print miss the mark entirely.

So, with a Dutch-English dictionary and my limited high school German, I began to decipher the diaries. I quickly saw how valuable they might be to a biographer, because they contain several pages on his escape to the Dutch sea coast and his early years in New York. Yet, all considered, I am having second thoughts about writing the biography. Do I really want to portray my uncle in all his complexity?

Among the illustrations we chose for display is Juliette's and my favorite, from *Félicien and the Vanishing Mountain,* the story in which in which Félicien, Gerard and Oscar – or I might say, Rudi, Dirk and Jaspar, and Thijs too, for his spirit is also there — discover a small mountain which has suddenly appeared in Central Park. The scene is at night under a clear, cobalt-blue sky in late March, lit only by the moon and the sweep of the Milky Way.

One senses a cold chill in the air, but also the promise and smell of spring. There is a look of awe on the faces of the beloved characters that captures the reason why children around the world love them so.

A deep sensibility haunts this painting, a longing for something beyond the tangible. In fact, there is a sense in which many of these illustrations touch on our most ancient memories. After all, what is more basic to our hearts than a night sky lit only by the moon and Milky Way or the scent and promise of spring on a clear and chilly night? It contains an echo of that night, when the moon lit up the country roads near Zuidveld as three boys went joy riding in a stolen luxury car and drank champagne, knowing they had outwitted the conqueror.

But I also think of the black times in Hans' life, the nightmares that fortunately find no echo in the *Félicien* stories – like that moment the interrogator sneers from across a table, the cries of the tortured rise and die in the air and a door waits for us at the end of the hall.

I sometimes recall the moment we found my uncle's body. He was sprawled on the ground, an odd look on his face, like that of a man who has been granted forgiveness. I was relieved. It was not at all the expression of a dying man who sees a dark hallway and a door waiting for him. The police took some time to examine the scene and then phoned the local medical authorities for assistance in removing the body. Finally, we headed back to the road. It was a long walk and I was moving slowly, reflecting on all that had happened. I found myself alone in a clearing when I heard the music, softly at first, then rising slightly. It sounded like a violin and a flute and the voice of a young woman singing. I looked about and re-traced my steps but could find nothing. And yet the music went on for minutes. Finally, it ceased and after a few puzzled moments, I turned and headed toward the road.

I cannot tell you today if the music was real or only fantasy playing a trick. And yet in a sense, this does not matter. I would like to imagine that the three fates were beckoning me at that moment as they had once to Hans, that a young woman was singing to me alone, that a flute was lifting my spirits and that a violin was crying out with a promise and a destiny that I might one day choose, or not, to pursue.

Hans had eventually said "yes" to his destiny and that promise. I did too, with Juliette's support, on the evening we unpacked the final box of Han's legacy, for then I was ready.

Manufactured by Amazon.ca
Bolton, ON